THE IMPOSSIBLE BOY

MARK GRIFFITHS

SIMON AND SCHUSTER

First published in Great Britain in 2014 by Simon and Schuster UK Ltd
A CBS COMPANY

1 3 5 7 9 10 8 6 4 2

Simon & Schuster UK Ltd
1st Floor
222 Gray's Inn Road
London WC1X 8HB

Simon & Schuster Australia, Sydney
Simon & Schuster India, New Delhi

A CIP catalogue record for this book
is available from the British Library.

PB ISBN: 978-0-85707-539-0
eBook ISBN: 978-0-85707-540-6

Printed and bound by CPI Group (UK) Ltd, Croydon, CRO 4YY

www.simonandschuster.co.uk
www.simonandschuster.com.au

FOR KATE SHAW – for making it possible.

With thanks to the Viney Agency,
Jane and Kat at Simon & Schuster,
Martin Chatterton and
Richard and Chloe Aldridge

PROLOGUE
THE ROBIN AND THE ROBOT
(BLUE HILLS: SATURDAY 7TH AUGUST 1976)

Shielding her eyes against the intense afternoon sunlight, the young girl stared in astonishment at the mayor and wondered why no one had noticed the ghost standing behind him.

A crowd of sixty or seventy people – couples with young children, mainly – had gathered in the small park to see the mayor open the new playground. Beside a gleaming set of swings, a tall metal slide and a gaudily painted roundabout, the mayor was reading a long, dreary speech into a microphone in his flat, plodding voice, his amplified words echoing away, dreamlike, into the hazy summer air. And, it seemed, not one person in the crowd was taking the slightest interest in the white, wraithlike form looming over his right shoulder. It was extremely odd, thought the girl.

The girl was eight years old, with a cascade of bright orange curls, and wore a faded set of tomboyish dungarees. Her name was Fleur Abbott. Wrinkling her freckly nose, she tugged at the sagging sleeve of her mother's dress. 'Look, Mum!' she hissed. 'There's a ghost! Can you see it?'

Mrs Abbott didn't respond. Her attention was focused entirely on the small silvery object in her hands. She was turning it over repeatedly, feeling every centimetre of its surface for some crack or seam like a hungry monkey trying to prise open a particularly tricky nut. She was frowning intensely, the tip of her tongue poking out through her teeth.

Fleur tugged at her sleeve again, without success. She let out a frustrated whine.

Fleur's father puffed on his pipe and snorted with laughter. Whitish smoke curled from his nostrils. 'Can't you put it down for ten seconds, my dear?' he said to his wife. 'I do believe our daughter is asking you a question.'

'I'm so close,' muttered Mrs Abbott, without looking up. 'I swear I felt the two halves come apart for a second. I bet there's some very simple trick to the locking mechanism And it's not like *you* could ever open it, with your big sausagey fingers.'

'How dare you!' gasped Mr Abbott in mock horror. 'I'll have you know I've got the fingers of a watchmaker.'

'Yes, a watchmaker with Cumberland sausages instead of normal fingers.'

Fleur giggled. Her dad's clumsy sausagelike fingers were a running joke in the Abbott family.

'I know you're fond of a puzzle, my sweet,' said Mr Abbot, 'but this is turning into an obsession. You've been fiddling with that thing non-stop since yesterday. Take a little break. It'll help clear your mind.' He took the object – a lozenge-shaped silver locket on a long silver chain – from her hands and slid it into the pocket of his cardigan. Mrs Abbott stuck out her tongue at him but said nothing. 'And anyway,' Mr Abbott continued, 'Fleur's found us a new mystery to investigate.' He winked at his daughter. 'Tell your mother what you've found, Fleur.'

Fleur pointed at the strange figure behind the mayor. 'Can you see it, Mum? The ghost?'

Mrs Abbott frowned. She raised her sunglasses and nestled them into her thick auburn hair. The figure was about five feet tall. It was draped in a white sheet and held its arms raised in a threatening stance like some evil phantom in a picture book or cartoon. 'Ah! I see it!' she announced 'But I don't think we'll need the services of an exorcist, after all.'

Fleur wrinkled her nose again. 'Does that mean it's not a ghost?'

'Afraid not, dear,' said Mr Abbott, patting his daughter on the shoulder.

'It's the statue that's been built to celebrate the new playground,' said Mrs Abbott. 'It's just covered by a sheet so the mayor can unveil it when he declares the playground open. Do you see now?'

Fleur looked at the white-draped figure again and pursed her lips. 'I suppose so,' she sighed. 'Pity. I'd like to see a real ghost one day.'

'Maybe you will, dear, one day,' said Mr Abbott, his pipe clenched between his teeth. 'The world is full of wonders. Your mother and I know that better than most people.'

Mrs Abbott nudged her husband. 'Tell Fleur about the mysterious presence we investigated in that guesthouse in Scotland the year before she was born. That's our best candidate for a real-life ghost.'

Mr Abbott chuckled delightedly. 'The Wandering Knight! Would you like to hear about that, Fleur? Some supernatural goings-on in the Highlands?'

Fleur's face brightened. 'Ooh, yes please! Tell me about a real ghost!'

Mr Abbott leaned forward and began to whisper into his daughter's ear. 'Once, about nine or ten years ago, your mother and I were staying in a guesthouse in a place in Scotland called Dufftown ...'

Fleur shivered with pleasure. She loved spooky stories – and Mr Abbott loved to tell them. Mrs Abbott knew this, of course, and while her husband was breathlessly recounting the story of the Wandering Knight to their daughter, she slipped her hand into the pocket of his cardigan and retrieved the locket without him noticing.

The mayor droned on. He thanked the company that had designed the new swings and slide and roundabout, which were, he assured the crowd, of the very latest and safest design. He thanked the council workers who had concreted over the three patches of grass for them to be placed on. He thanked a man called Bigglesby, who had lent him a pen when he first had the idea of building a new playground in the park and needed to make a note in case he forgot. And finally, he thanked a local artist by the name of Fiona Cress, who had made the delightful statue that he just knew children would love and which he was now about to unveil, declaring, as he did so, that this new playground was well and truly open.

With a flourish, he whipped the sheet away from the statue.

There was a second or two of silence while the crowd, a little numbed by the heat of the day and the length of the mayor's speech, realised that he had stopped speaking. This was filled promptly by a burst of grateful applause and even a few cheers.

'Look!' cried Fleur, jabbing an excited finger at the statue. 'Cluedroid! And that's Bobby Robin with him! It's *The Robin and the Robot* from the TV show!'

Annoyed at this interruption to his story (he had just been getting to the good bit about the axe), Mr Abbott frowned at the statue. In grey-speckled whitish granite, he saw a roughly human-shaped robot figure dressed in the traditional long overcoat and broad-brimmed hat of a private detective. Both the robot's arms were raised at shoulder height, its left hand open in a friendly wave. The palm of its right hand was flat and on it sat a plump granite robin, perky, with a mischievous look in its tiny round eyes. The left leg of the robot was raised and resting on a large square sign – the kind that might hang outside a detective's office and into which the words *The Robin and the Robot* had been carved in space-age letters.

'I see,' said Mr Abbott. 'And what exactly do the Robin and the Robot do on their show? I suppose they solve all sorts of whimsical and unlikely mysteries together, eh?' grinned Mr Abbott. 'Am I right?'

Fleur winced. '*Well* ... it's a *bit* more complicated than that ...'

'Got it!' cried Mrs Abbott as the locket in her hands finally came open.

The sudden flash of white light caught everyone off guard. When the mayor later recalled it, he compared it to the time in 1954 when he had witnessed an atomic bomb test on a remote Pacific island. He had the same feeling then that the entire world was suddenly dissolving into burning whiteness, as if plunged into the heart of the sun. Many said they remembered covering their eyes with their hands and being able to see the bones in their fingers as clear as an X-ray as the savage light blasted through them. For a few brief seconds, it was as if all life, all consciousness, was extinguished in the merciless glare. The only thing that existed was the white light.

Mr Abbott blinked, a procession of shapeless black after-images jigging before his eyes. What on Earth had just happened? Had a bomb gone off? There had been no sound of an explosion, only the overpowering light. Had he been deafened? No, he realised. He could hear the startled gasps and moans of those around him. In time his vision cleared and he saw his wife before him, open-mouthed in utter confusion.

'What the hell was that?' she groaned. Her voice was hoarse. She adjusted the sunglasses in her hair with trembling fingers.

Mr Abbott shrugged dumbly. Instinctively he went to place his hands on Fleur's shoulders. The pipe dropped from his mouth and landed softly on the grass. He looked around, suddenly wild-eyed, his heart thumping, his thick-fingered hands clasping and unclasping anxiously. 'Where's Fleur?' he asked his wife, a tiny tremor in his voice.

CHAPTER ONE
THE AMAZING CHAS HINTON
(BLUE HILLS: PRESENT DAY)

Barney Watkins was quaking with rage.

He clenched his fists, the skin on his knuckles turning a translucent yellow-white, as he stomped through the open door into classroom U13. Eleven years old, with a snub nose and a flick of shiny black hair, he was the kind of kid, average in seemingly every way, that people instantly forgot the moment he left the room. He sighed long and hard, his breath escaping like steam fizzing from a volcano.

His friend Gabby Grayling was waiting for him in the room with a girl he didn't recognise. The girl was about his age, with long dark hair and a pale complexion.

'Barney,' said Gabby, 'this is Laura. She—'

'You won't believe what ridiculous old Mr Jones has done!' interrupted Barney. 'Urgh. He makes me ... So. Flipping. Angry.'

Gabby blinked at him and adjusted her small round glasses on her nose. She had curly brown hair and big dark eyes that seemed to swallow you whole. A couple of years older than Barney, she often felt a little protective of him. 'What happened, mate?'

'He just confiscated my EGG!'

Gabby shrugged. 'So what? It's lunchtime. We'll get some food from the canteen later.'

Barney moaned as if in pain. 'Not that sort of egg, Gabby! An *E-G-G*. Electronic Gaming Globe? It's a vintage hand-held video game. From the

1970s. I got it from a charity shop in Kent last year. I brought it in to show Lewis and Mr Jones caught us looking at it in maths and now he's confiscated it, put it in that stupid old safe he has at the back of his classroom! *The Black Hole*, everyone calls it. Once stuff ends up in there it never sees the light of day again!'

'Tough break, mate,' said Gabby, trying to look sympathetic and not making a terribly good job of it. 'A major injustice, I'm sure. We'll figure out a way to get it back later. But can we get on with some Geek Inc. business? Laura has just told me something that could need further investigation.'

Geek Inc. was a school club run by Barney and Gabby and devoted to investigating the impossible. That was the idea, anyway. When Barney had first joined the club about two months ago – being new to Blue Hills High School, lonely, and in need of something to do at lunchtimes – Gabby (the club's only other member, a fact that she'd not mentioned until Barney had already agreed to join) had implied that they would spend all their time chasing ghosts and investigating flying saucers. This had so far, somewhat conspicuously, failed to happen. There had been one genuinely strange incident, shortly after he had joined, involving a secret government formula that brought inanimate objects to life. But since then, nothing.

Since their first investigation, Barney and Gabby had tried to encourage kids at Blue Hills High to come forward with any reports of strange happenings for Geek Inc. to look into, but all of these had turned out to be much less odd than they first appeared. A 'sea monster' in the canal was revealed to be no more than a cardboard cut-out of a dinosaur thrown in by the manager of the town's bookshop to generate publicity for a 'monster sale' he was planning. He was fined for littering. A 'vampire postman' kids reported seeing on the way to school was just an ordinary, if somewhat paler than normal, postman with a habit of drinking tomato juice on the job. And tales of a werewolf stalking the town's bowling green every full moon were found to be outright lies spread by a pensioner with too much time on his hands.

The business with the government formula had briefly shown Barney that the world could be a much weirder and more remarkable place than he had ever imagined. But since then normal life, with its unchanging routine of school, homework, football practice and nagging parents, had quickly reasserted itself and he had started to wonder if anything out of the ordinary would ever happen to him again.

He raised his eyebrows at Gabby. 'This had better be really, *really* good because I'm not in the mood for any more time-wasters.'

Gabby looked at Laura. 'Can you tell Barney what you told me?'

Laura crossed her arms and fixed Barney with a

confidential, big-eyed stare. '*Well,*' she said in a strong Blue Hills accent, 'there's this *lad* in my class, right? He's *new*. Only started here two weeks ago. *Seems* normal, like an *ordinary* kid, right? *But ...*'

'Go on,' said Barney.

'Get this ...' said Laura. She paused dramatically.

'Yes?'

'He's *always* got a pen on him.'

Barney blinked. 'What?' He frowned and looked at Gabby. She was grinning.

'I mean *always*,' said Laura. 'Absolutely *always*. It's well weird.'

Barney raised a palm to his face. 'Really? Great. Well done both of you for a great wind-up. Ha ha. How very, very clever. Now if you don't mind I'm going to go and grovel to Mr Jones to see if there's anything I can do to get my EGG back because, believe it or not, I do actually have better things to do than stand here being treated like some kind of idiot by a pair of smirking *girls*.' He turned on his heel, tie swinging, face prickling with heat.

'Wait!' called Gabby. There was laughter in her voice. 'Barney! Stop! This is a real mystery! Honestly!'

'You think?' said Barney, turning to face her from the doorway. 'A boy always having a pen counts as a real mystery now, does it? Seems to me like the standard of oddness we're prepared to investigate in this club has declined a bit, Gabs. What's our next case going to be? *The Strange Affair of the Sausage Roll That When Someone Ate It They Felt Less Hungry? The Mysterious Case of the Grass That Was Green?*'

'Please wait,' said Gabby. 'There is actually more to this. I promise.'

Barney shot her a sceptical look. 'Well?' he asked, leaning against the doorway and folding his arms.

Gabby touched Laura's elbow. 'Tell him the rest.'

Laura grinned. 'OK. Here's the thing, right? I say he's always got a pen on him. I mean, *really*, always. It's like a magic trick he does. He can produce a pen out of nowhere. *Literally.* I've seen him do it. Like, three or four times in our English class before the teacher arrived. There's nothing in his hands, *nothing.* He rolls his sleeves up so you can see he hasn't got anything hidden up them. Then he flicks a wrist and there's a pen *right there* in his hand. A proper biro, not a fake paper biro that he could hide between his fingers or anything. He can make pens appear out of nowhere. I swear. It's like he's *properly* magic.' She nodded to emphasise this last point.

Barney scratched his chin slowly. He had calmed down a bit now.

'What do you think?' Gabby asked him.

Barney shrugged. 'So he knows a magic trick? With a bit of practice, I could probably do the same thing.'

'But,' said Gabby, 'if this boy is really doing it the way Laura's describing – nothing up his sleeves, totally empty hands – it sounds pretty impossible to me.'

'*If* that's really how he does it,' said Barney. 'And it all depends on that one little word *if*, doesn't it?' He looked at Laura. 'Who is he, anyway?'

'He's called Chas Hinton,' said Laura.

'Chas Hinton?' repeated Barney with a smirk. 'I know Chas. He's in my maths class! We were both just in Mr Jones's lesson. He was sitting about three desks away from me.'

'You know him?' said Gabby. 'What's he like?'

'He's *all right*, I suppose,' said Barney. 'He's always making people laugh. Most people like him. Actually, everyone likes him. He's dead popular. Which is a bit weird because he hasn't been at Blue Hills High very long.'

'Is that a note of jealousy in your voice, Barney?' asked Gabby.

Barney flushed. 'Of course not. So Chas is brilliant and wonderful and everyone adores him. Good for him. But there's nothing actually *magical* about him.'

'Laura seems to think there is,' said Gabby. 'It's got to be worth looking into, though, don't you think?'

Barney screwed up his face. 'Yeah, OK. Why not? I suppose we've been a bit short on things to investigate lately anyway. We can't afford to be all that choosy.' He turned to Laura. 'I don't suppose you've noticed anything else strange about Chas, have you? Any other little tricks he gets up to?'

'I have, actually, now you ask,' said Laura. 'I was going to mention it but it slipped my mind.'

'What is it?' asked Barney.

'He can walk on water.'

They searched the playground but there was no sign of Chas. None of the kids they asked seemed to know where he was. They were about to give up when Barney had an idea.

'Follow me,' he said. He sounded decisive.

The two girls exchanged a glance and followed.

'Tell us about the water thing again,' he said to Laura. 'In a bit more detail, please.'

Laura shrugged. 'It was last week. In PE. The boys' class had just come out of the swimming pool and I was with the rest of the girls queued up outside waiting to go in. I was first in the queue. I looked through and I could see the lads getting out of the pool, going in their changing room. The last one out was Chas. He was just about to go in the changing room when their teacher, Mr Ross, calls to Chas and tells him to fetch his whistle and his clipboard, which he's left at the side of the diving board, right?'

'OK . . .?'

'So, Chas looks around, making sure there's no one there to see him – he doesn't know I'm watching from the other doorway, of course – and then, instead of walking around the pool to get Mr Ross's gear, he walks *across* it! Right across the surface of the water! He grabs the whistle and the clipboard and then he walks back the same way, *on the water*. Just like he's walking on the ground. It was *well* weird!'

'Why didn't you mention this earlier?' asked Barney. 'Isn't walking on water a few thousand times more impossible than doing some magic trick with a pen?'

Laura looked slightly shamefaced. 'Forgot, didn't I? I was gonna tell my mate Sharleen about it. She was standing right next to me in the queue for the pool, but before I could, she turns to me and tells me this *amazing* bit of gossip about Fran Milton in Year Nine. It was awesome gossip – I'd tell you what it was, but I'm sworn to secrecy – and the thing with Chas walking on the water just went totally out of my mind.'

Barney spluttered. 'You saw someone walk on water and you forgot all about it because your friend told you some *gossip*?'

'You don't understand,' said Laura. 'This was pretty awesome gossip.'

'It must have been,' said Barney. He shook his head and looked at Gabby, expecting to find her as incredulous as him, but was astonished to find her giggling instead.

He led them around a corner to the back of the school canteen where he knew there was a wheelchair ramp leading up to a fire door. The area was hidden from the main part of the playground, making it the perfect venue for dodgy activity. And it was here, standing on the wheelchair ramp, that they found Chas Hinton. A crowd of about ten kids from all years had gathered around him. They were applauding.

'Thank you, kindly! Thank you! Cheers m'dears!' said Chas in a loud, friendly voice. He was a tall boy with straight blond hair parted to one side. He wore it very long at the front so that one eye was permanently obscured by a curtain of hair.

Barney and the two girls stood a few feet behind the audience and watched. Gabby prodded Barney with a finger. He raised his eyebrows at her. She leaned in close. For a horrified second he thought she was going to kiss him there and then in the playground. 'By the way,' she said in a low voice, 'can I just say, over the past few weeks I've seen you really blossom into quite the investigator. The Barney I met back at the start of term would never have taken command of this case and thrown himself into investigating it with such gusto. Well done, mate.'

'Oh,' said Barney, face flushing. 'Thanks, Gabs. Well, what can I say? I learned from the best.'

'Really?' said Gabby. 'Aw!' She beamed at him, her big eyes shining.

'Yeah,' said Barney, 'I've been reading my dad's Sherlock Holmes books. That guy's a genius.'

Gabby's face froze. She recovered herself quickly and flashed him a tight-lipped smile. 'Oh, yeah, yeah. They're great books.' She turned away.

'I'm really getting into them,' continued Barney. 'Sherlock Holmes is a great investigator. I was thinking of writing to him for some advice – you know, about our cases.'

Gabby emitted a strange snorting sound.

'You OK?'

'Fine,' said Gabby. 'Fine. Touch of hay fever.'

'In November?'

'Yeah, weird huh?'

The applause ceased. Chas bowed modestly. 'For his next act of perplexing prestidigitation,' he boomed in a comical posh voice, 'the amazing Chas Hinton requires the assistance of a member of the audience. Who's up for a dangerous dabble with the dark arts? Which of you fancies a fiddle with some forbidden fruit? Who among you has the intellect to interrogate the intricacies of the inexplicable?' He scanned the crowd, a hand shading his eyes. 'Ah!' he exclaimed. 'There's a familiar face! I do believe it's Mr Barney Watkins from my maths class! Would you care to help me out, Barney?'

'Me?' mouthed Barney, pointing at himself.

Gabby shoved him forward. 'Go for it,' she hissed in his ear. 'This is your chance to scrutinise his act up close.'

'A big hand for Mr Barney Watkins!' cried Chas. The crowd of kids clapped, parting to let him through. Gabby stuck two fingers in her mouth and emitted a piercing whistle. Barney joined Chas at the top of the wheelchair ramp.

'Now then,' said Chas, 'let's see if we can't rustle up a little magic for Barney here, eh? And what better way to go about the business of rustling than with ... *a paper bag*?' With an extravagant gesture he drew a brown paper bag from his trouser pocket and handed it to Barney. 'Be so good as to check the bag if you would, Barney. Look inside it – check for any hidden trapdoors, rabbits or mirrors. Show it to the audience. You will see that it is a perfectly normal brown paper bag in every conceivable way.'

Barney examined it. It was an ordinary paper bag of the type used by the school tuck shop. It was completely empty. He held it up for the others to see. As he did so he had the nagging feeling that while he and the audience's attention was focused on the bag, Chas was probably subtly fiddling with all kinds of secret props and stuff unnoticed – the magician's true art being in misdirection. He hoped Gabby was keeping an eye on Chas and not the bag.

'Satisfied that it's completely normal?'

Barney nodded. 'Yup.'

Chas made great show of rolling up the sleeves

of his jumper and shirt, revealing his pale, freckle-daubed forearms. He fanned his hands elegantly. His fingers were extraordinarily long and supple. 'As you can see, there is nothing up my sleeves or in my hands. Now, Barney – the bag, if you will?' He held out a hand and Barney passed him the paper bag. As he did so, Chas slipped a hand into his pocket and handed a very small metal object to Barney. Barney stared at it. 'A pin!' said Chas. 'Its purpose will become clear in a moment.' He gathered the neck of the paper bag and raised it to his lips, inflating it like a balloon with a single big gust of breath. Carefully prising the neck shut between thumb and forefinger, he handed the inflated paper bag to Barney. 'Now,' said Chas, 'you're going to do this trick, Barney. I want you to hold the paper bag in one hand and, after the count of three, I want you to pop it like a balloon with the pin. You got that?'

Barney nodded. 'Yep.'

Chas winked theatrically at Barney. 'Let's see what happens, eh?' He turned to the audience. 'Everyone – *one, two* ...'

The crowd joined in enthusiastically with the count. Barney could make out Gabby's voice distinctly.

'*Three!*'

The watching kids held their breath.

Barney thrust the pin into the inflated paper bag.

There was a loud popping sound, followed by the rapid thudding of wings. Two perfect snow-white doves soared out of the paper bag in a shower of brightly coloured confetti. Barney felt an object drop into his hands. The two doves alighted on the roof of the canteen, lingered a moment, and then climbed high into the overcast sky.

'Two beautiful birds!' exclaimed Chas. 'And it seems one has left a little present for Mr Watkins!'

The audience went wild with hoots and cheers. Barney looked dumbly at the object in his hands as the coloured dots of confetti fluttered to the ground all around him. His jaw dropped open. There, stuck to the back of the object was the small, faded Smurf sticker that Barney had attached to it years ago. That confirmed it. It was definitely his. He stared at Chas, wide-eyed. 'This is my EGG! I thought I'd never see it again! How did you get it?'

'Barney!' said Chas in quiet tones of mock-horror. 'What kind of magician would I be if I revealed my secrets?'

CHAPTER TWO
THE MESSAGE

Edgar Lyndhurst rapped a knuckle on the polished oak door. The noise reverberated for a long time before dying away into ominous silence. He held his breath while he waited for a reply. Tiny beads of sweat were forming on his forehead. His hands felt icy cold and faintly damp.

It wasn't every day you knocked on the door of the eighth most powerful man in the world.

Edgar was fiftyish, balding, with big thick-rimmed glasses and the kind of nose that made his colleagues whisper things behind his back – things like 'anteater', 'proboscis monkey' and, in the case of one exceptionally unimaginative person, 'Edgar's got a *very* big nose, hasn't he?' He was wearing a trim and tasteful dark suit and clutched in one of his clammy-palmed hands was a tiny scrap of paper. In his ears, his pulse throbbed.

He was standing in a sombre windowless corridor, some thirty metres under the pavement of central London. It was in a part of Secret Service headquarters he had never visited before, a grey, unadorned place he had until this afternoon believed to be no more than an unused storeroom. A buzzer sounded and a notice situated directly above the door suddenly illuminated. It said simply, *ENTER*.

Taking a deep breath, Edgar turned the handle and swung open the door.

The room he stepped into was roughly half the size of a football pitch. Its bare concrete floor stretched away before him into the dim distance.

The high ceiling was hung with dim bare light bulbs, which cast small circular pools of tepid yellowish light at regular intervals. In the distance, in the centre of this vast room, he could make out a small desk, its surface completely bare, behind which there sat a man.

As he approached, Edgar became aware that he had made a miscalculation of scale. The desk was much bigger than it had seemed. In fact, as he drew closer, it looked like it might be the size of a smallish tennis court. The man behind it seemed correspondingly bigger too. He was a round-faced bull of a chap, surprisingly young – possibly even still in his twenties – with large pink jowls and an abundance of untidy yellow hair. He was sitting very grandly on what seemed to be a cross between an office swivel chair and a throne. From this he looked down on Edgar like the god of some remote mountaintop and bestowed upon him a generous smile.

'Can I help you?' he boomed. Such were the acoustics in this massive room that it was scarcely possible to speak any other way. His voice was rich and fruity and its owner obviously enjoyed the sound of it very much.

'I have a ... that is, I've brought – a ... a message,' Edgar stammered. His throat was suddenly very dry. He stared at the scrap of paper in his hands. 'From F Section. They considered it too ... uh ... *sensitive* to trust to email. So they've sent me.'

'I see,' said the man calmly. 'And what might this message be?'

'Here.' Edgar held out the scrap of paper.

The man behind the desk tutted. 'No, no, no! Even the tiniest piece of paper can end up in the hands of those who are not supposed to see it, can it not? Do it the proper Secret Service way. Memorise the words, eat the paper, and then repeat the words to me. Understood?'

Edgar eyed the tiny scrap of paper in his hands. It was moist from his own sweat, its edges starting to curl. There was a grubby thumbprint in one corner. 'The thing is,' Edgar began, 'I had rather a big breakfast this morning, so if it's all the same to you, can I just read you what–'

'It is NOT all the same to me!' exclaimed the man behind the desk. His voice resounded like an angry kettledrum. 'I gave you an order, man! Memorise, eat, repeat! Now get on with it!'

Edgar sighed. He read the words on the paper one more time, even though he already knew them by heart, and folded the paper into a tiny square. He popped it in his mouth, where it lay on his tongue as dry and tasteless as a headache tablet. With a great effort he swallowed it, his whole body shuddering.

The man behind the desk watched with satisfaction. 'Good. Now. The message!'

Edgar opened his mouth to speak, but found his

mind was utterly blank. There was a second of sickening blackness during which he imagined what unspeakable punishments the man behind the desk might subject him to for forgetting the message – and then the words suddenly popped back into his mind. He got them out quickly in case they disappeared again. 'The message says, "Magpie 94 has detected small quantities of Harland radiation in multiple UK sites." That's it. That's all it said. Erm … thank you.' He gave a sharp dry cough. The scrap of paper seemed to be taking a very long time to work its way down his throat.

'Thank you very much indeed. That's extremely interesting. A moment, please.'

The man pushed a button on the arm of his chair. With a near-silent electric whir, a small hatch opened on the surface of the gigantic desk and a tiny laptop computer no bigger than a paperback book slid smoothly out. The man now typed slowly and daintily at its miniature keyboard with his surprisingly small, girlish fingers. Light from the laptop's tiny screen flickered across his face.

Edgar glanced around the gigantic room. It was more like an aircraft hangar than an office. He didn't envy whoever had to clean it.

The eyes of the man behind the desk flicked upwards at Edgar and then returned to the screen. 'You are wondering about this office, I can tell. You are curious about its size and apparent emptiness, are you not?'

Edgar shrugged as casually as he could. 'Your working arrangements are no concern of mine, I'm quite sure.'

'Oh come off it. You're only human, man! It's natural to be inquisitive. One expects it of Secret Service personnel.' The man fixed him with a stare. 'This office was once a storeroom, you know. It used to be filled to the rafters with blankets, medical supplies, bottled water, canned food, biscuits–'

'I'm a big fan of biscuits,' chipped in Edgar, happy to have found a subject on which he could speak with authority. 'I'm a custard-cream man myself. Fantastic biscuit. Charlotte – she's my wife, we've just celebrated our thirtieth anniversary – Charlotte and I visited the factory in Yorkshire where they make them and it was by far the best biscuit factory tour we've ever been on. And we've been on a few!'

The man grunted, but whether it was in agreement with Edgar's comment or merely in annoyance at being interrupted, he couldn't tell.

'In short,' the man continued, 'there were enough supplies in here to keep a few dozen people alive for, well, potentially, years. It was the storeroom for the government's secret nuclear bunker, you see. In the event of a nuclear attack on London – back in the days when such a thing was deemed likely – Britain's top brass were all meant to hide down here and wait it out. Lucky them, eh?' He chuckled macabrely at the thought. 'That was all in the bad old days, of course, and the world is a considerably safer place nowadays, thanks largely to the efforts of people like you and me. Or more specifically,' the man smiled, '*me.*'

Edgar smiled politely. 'I have no doubt.'

'You see,' said the man, 'I have quite recently enjoyed something of a promotion. A few brief months ago I was a mere drone at the Ministry of Defence. Just another bumbling clod working on the usual top secret technology stuff. But after some pretty darn clever manoeuvrings on my part – largely due to my handling of some recent odd business at a school in Blue Hills – I'm now a far more important number here at the Secret Service. Or rather,' and here he grinned a slow catlike grin, 'somewhat *above* the Secret Service. I have tasted power and – by Jove, sir – *I like it.* By the way, did you know that I am the eighth most powerful person in the entire world?'

Edgar nodded. 'I had heard.'

The man looked disappointed. 'Oh. Anyway, my job is basically to stop the Prime Minister of Great Britain worrying about the state of the world, about the prospect of wars, of revolutions, of threats of all kinds. Anything that would make him want to scurry for safety underground and fill up this storeroom again. So you see, as long as this room remains empty, I am doing my job. And the PM doesn't care in the *slightest* how I go about it.'

Edgar nodded. 'Of course.' He had worked for the Secret Service for nearly twenty years and knew there was scarcely a single foul deed they would not commit in the pursuit of Britain's interests.

The man rose to his feet and walked around to the front of the desk. The desk being the size it was, this took a good ten seconds. He held out his hands graciously to Edgar.

'Thank you so much for coming here today with

the message. I do appreciate your taking the trouble. I'm so sorry I was snippy with you earlier.'

He shook Edgar warmly by the hand, clasping his other hand tightly over Edgar's.

'Not at all,' said Edgar. 'We're both just doing our jobs.' He felt a sudden sharp pricking in the back of his hand. He snatched it out of the man's grip. There was a red dot on the back of his hand. Blood.

'Forgive me,' said the man. Edgar saw he was holding a small, stubby syringe in the hand he had clasped over his. 'A sedative. And rather a powerful one too.'

'Whuh ...?' Edgar's vision suddenly began to blur.

'You see,' said the man, 'the thing is, you saw the message. And the fewer people who see it, the better for Britain. Thankfully though, the sedative now entering your system will erase all memory of your visit here today.'

'Whuh . . . ?' said Edgar again. His mouth wasn't working terribly well. Or his limbs. He sank slowly to his knees.

'In fact, I'm afraid that, as we can take no chances with the security of the message, to be on the safe side I had to give you a dose of the sedative so strong that it will erase your memory of the entire last – oooh – twenty-five, thirty years, I should think.'

'Thirty years?' mumbled Edgar. His lips were numb. The floor suddenly looked like a very comfortable place. He lay on it, cradling his head in his hands.

'I believe you mentioned you were married?' said the man.

Edgar nodded dumbly. He tried to mouth the word 'Charlotte'.

'Splendid! Complete amnesia is the perfect way to put the sparkle back into your relationship! All those years of arguments and nagging swept away in an instant. You'll be able to get to know each other all over again. I'm really most jealous!'

Edgar did not reply because he was no longer conscious.

The man returned to his thronelike chair and pressed a button on the armrest. A second small hatch opened on the vast surface of the desk and a tiny telephone no bigger than a playing card slid upwards. The keypad of the phone bore only a single digit – 1. He gently pressed the number with a finger and held the tiny phone to his ear. There was a muted ringing tone.

'Hello?' said a voice.

'Good afternoon!' said the man cheerfully. He eyed Edgar's unconscious form. 'I wonder if you might send a cleaner over to the office? It appears to be somewhat ... er ... *untidy*.'

'Certainly, sir. Be about five minutes.'

'Thank you!' said Sir Orville McIntyre. 'You really are most terribly kind.'

CHAPTER THREE
CHAS CHASE

Gabby pressed herself flat against the wall, feeling the rough brickwork scrape against the back of her head. She checked her watch. School was due to finish in just under three minutes.

This time she wouldn't lose him.

The previous afternoon, she and Barney had met up in a quiet corner of the playground during break time to discuss the strange magical abilities of Chas Hinton.

'You've got to admit, mate,' said Gabby, removing her small, round glasses and cleaning them with the edge of her jumper, 'that trick with the doves was pretty darn cool. I can't begin to imagine how he does it. And the way he works the audience! He's so charming, isn't he? I can see why everyone likes him.'

'In other words, he's a show-off who knows a few magic tricks,' said Barney, rolling his eyes. 'Biiiiiiig deal! Hardly impossible, though, is it?'

Gabby smiled and slotted her glasses back on to her nose. 'What about him walking on water, then? If that's a trick, I wouldn't mind learning it. It would make going on holiday to France a lot cheaper if you could hike there!'

Barney wrinkled his nose. 'We've only got Laura's word for that, haven't we? She might have made a mistake. Or she could be lying.'

'Why on Earth would she want to lie about Chas walking on water?'

Barney shrugged. 'People do the weirdest things to get attention, don't they? Back in Kent an old lady on our street used to tell everyone that elves were stealing her tea bags. She was on the local TV news saying she'd stayed up one night to take a photo of them doing it but she'd put her thumb over the camera lens by mistake and none of the pictures came out. She was talking rubbish, obviously, but it got her on the telly, didn't it? Maybe it's the same with Laura.'

'She hardly seems the type to invent stuff,' said Gabby, 'and she's a pretty popular girl herself – it's not like she's short of attention.'

'We need to find out more about Chas,' said Barney. 'I don't know where he's from, what his folks do. Anything about his life outside school. Discovering that might give us some clue.'

'I'll ask around,' said Gabby. 'Someone might know something.'

'And I'm going to follow him home tonight. See

where he lives. We're in the same general science class for last lesson today.'

'You could always just, you know, ask him where he's from,' said Gabby with a teasing smile. 'Engage him in conversation. It's a pretty good way to find out stuff about people, believe it or not.'

Barney shook his head. 'I don't want him to know we're investigating him. He might try to mislead us. I know everyone thinks he's ace but there's something about him I don't like. I don't trust him.'

Gabby widened her eyes in mock-terror. 'Oh no! Take care following him then, mate! Do you want me to come along and act as your bodyguard in case things turn ugly?'

'Ha flipping ha,' said Barney in a flat voice. 'Don't worry about me, Gabs. I reckon I'm pretty good at following people without being noticed. You'll see.'

When the bell rang at three-thirty that afternoon at the end of the general science lesson, Barney calmly put his things back in his schoolbag, keeping one eye firmly on Chas Hinton, who was sitting a couple of desks in front of him. Chas slid from his seat, pulled on his coat and headed for the door. Barney followed silently.

Chas rounded a corner, moving against the flow of bodies streaming towards the main entrance, and slipped into the school hall. Barney could see him clearly through the window in one of the hall's wide double-doors. He was walking towards the centre of the empty hall. *Interesting* ...

'See you at football practice on Thursday night, Barney?'

It was a boy called Rob Yellowwood, a tall kid with red hair and a freckly nose.

'What?' said Barney. 'Oh yeah, sure. Sorry, mate. Can't talk now. Need to be somewhere. See you Thursday.' He waved absently at Rob and quickly sidled up to the double-doors leading into the hall. He peered inside.

It was completely empty.

Frowning, Barney pulled open the door and stepped inside, his footsteps echoing on the wooden floor. His eyes darted around the empty hall, his heart sinking lower with every step. He checked behind the headmaster's lectern, behind the piano; he checked every inch of floor, every corner of the room. There were no other exits. Nowhere to hide.

It had happened. He had, in that briefest of moments, lost Chas. It was impossible. But he had managed it. And now Gabby was going to know just how rubbish at investigating he was ...

'Don't worry about it, mate,' Gabby laughed later that evening when he phoned to tell her about his investigative blunder. 'I'm sure even Sherlock Holmes had an off day.'

Next day, though, was different. Gabby was prepared. She had a *plan*. And as Barney was away from school on his LifeSkillz placement, she was also on her own and would have no one else to blame if she messed up.

LifeSkillz was a scheme dreamed up by Mr Steele, the deputy head at Blue Hills High, to get pupils involved in their local community and give them a glimpse of life outside the classroom. Mr Steele himself had come up with the name 'LifeSkillz' – he was very keen on the 'z'; kids liked words with 'z's in them, apparently – and for two afternoons a week the kids (or as Mr Steele put it, 'the kidz') in Barney's year were assigned to people, places and institutions in Blue Hills that needed a little assistance. Some kids got to help out at *The Blue Hills Weekly Chronicle*, some at the local radio station. Barney, however, had been assigned to help out an elderly couple who lived near the school, something, if he was honest, he wasn't too happy about.

Faking an optician's appointment, Gabby had

left her final lesson of the day twenty minutes early. She used this time to slip into the girls' toilets and change into a different coat and a curly blonde wig she had bought the previous year for a fancy dress party (she had gone as Marilyn Monroe but everyone had assumed she was Lady Gaga, much to her annoyance). She removed her glasses and put in her emergency contact lenses. The tiny slivers of plastic felt weird and uncomfortable in her eyes but she knew any disguise she donned would be useless if she was still wearing her usual glasses. An old baseball cap pulled down low over her face completed the outfit.

That morning, Laura had told her which classroom Chas would be in for his final lesson of the day – class LO5 (the LO stood for Lower Block, a long single-storey building that was the oldest in the school). Laura had also told her that kids in her and Chas's form were not doing their LifeSkillz activities until next term so he should definitely be in school today. Gabby had a sudden vision of Chas on LifeSkillz working on the checkout in a supermarket and making customers' groceries vanish as they trundled along the conveyor belt. She stifled a giggle.

The school bell rang. Gabby tensed. From within the building erupted the happy shouts and laughter that signalled the end of the school day, followed by the weary voices of teachers calling for calm. Chairs scraped against the floor. Fire doors squeaked and slammed. Muffled footsteps echoed down corridors. And then, like cola from a well-shaken can, a stream of kids burst through the door of the Lower Block and exploded into the playground, yelling, running, pulling on their coats, all with a single happy thought – *home*.

Chas was one of the first kids out. He waved at another boy and sauntered towards the school gate. Gabby followed, moving through the crowd at a leisurely pace, keeping her distance.

Watching Chas move through the school gates, Gabby pushed forwards and, pulling down the peak of her cap further still, she followed.

Town was clogged with traffic. Cars and buses were bunched up against one another like impatient cattle, engines grumbling and exhausts coughing out streams of smelly white clouds. Gabby slid into the doorway of a shop and peeped around at Chas. He was standing outside a specialist hi-fi shop a few doors down, gazing in at various pieces of unidentifiable matte black audio equipment. *What is it about boys and hi-fi stuff?* she wondered. Could anyone really tell the difference between a CD player that cost thirty pounds and one that cost three thousand pounds?

Then a thought struck her.

She remembered reading somewhere that a lot of the specialist props that magicians used in their tricks were actually extremely expensive pieces of high technology. An apparently simple bit of conjuring involving, for instance, some vanishing sponge balls might actually utilise cutting-edge materials and techniques developed by big electronics corporations or even NASA to achieve its effects. Perhaps Chas was somehow using the science of sound to influence people's minds and this was why he was so interested in state-of-the-art audio equipment? Could sounds of a certain frequency interfere with a person's brainwaves and make them hallucinate that they'd seen miraculous feats? It seemed doubtful, she thought – impossible even – but that was what Geek Inc. was all about, wasn't it? Maybe if she could see which bits of audio gear Chas was looking at that might give her some clue? She stepped out of the doorway, her eyes fixed on Chas …

'Ooof!'

The old lady in the fur coat slammed into Gabby with the force of a rugby fullback. The two of them tumbled to the ground in a jumble of limbs. Gabby leaped to her feet, half dazed, gabbling frantic apologies, and attempted to help her up.

'Keep away!' bellowed the old lady, waving her umbrella at Gabby. She was a squat, white-haired creature with a sour little mouth and fierce glasses. The skin sagging from her neck reminded Gabby of an old tortoise she once owned. 'You won't get my purse, you little thug!'

'I'm not a thug,' objected Gabby, one eye on Chas and trying to keep her voice down. The last thing she needed now was to attract his attention. 'I'm just a girl. I'm so sorry. Here, let me help you ... Yowch!' The old lady's umbrella slashed through the air like a sword. Gabby snatched back her stinging hand. 'Hey! That really hurt! I was only trying to help you up!'

'Only trying to help yourself to my pension, more like!' squawked the old lady, struggling to her feet. 'Help!' she screeched. 'Police! I'm being mugged! This is a hate crime! Old people have rights too, you know!'

'I'm not mugging you!' hissed Gabby. 'I swear! Please stop shouting! There's really nothing to be afraid of.' She almost put her hand over the old lady's mouth but thankfully thought better of it. Instead, she put her arm around her shoulder and guided her gently into the doorway of the shop out of view of the rest of the street.

'Listen to me,' said Gabby, speaking very slowly and clearly. 'It was just an accident, that's all. And you're OK, aren't you? You're not actually hurt in any way.'

'As a matter of fact,' said the old lady curtly, 'I *am* hurt. You've broken my leg.'

'Broken your leg?' hissed Gabby through clenched teeth. 'You're standing up! You wouldn't be doing that if your leg was broken.' She could feel the anger rising inside herself like steam in a kettle. Why was she standing here arguing with this potty old woman when she had a mission to carry out?

'Well, it certainly feels broken,' insisted the old lady, rubbing her leg. 'Or at the very least badly bruised. Either way I shall be doing my best to ensure that you are put behind bars for many, many years for the wicked crime you have committed today. And listen to me when I'm telling you off, won't you? Stop gawping into the distance! What are you looking for? Your manners?'

'Hmm?' muttered Gabby absently, as she tried to peer over the old lady's shoulder. She was pretty sure Chas was still there ...

A woman emerged from the shop. She was squat like the old lady, burly, with short hair dyed a very bright shade of red. She eyed Gabby, her face stony. 'What's going on 'ere, Mum?' she asked the old lady in a gruff voice.

'This young tearaway has just assaulted me and tried to rob me blind! Pin her down while I fetch the police.'

The woman with the red hair rolled her eyes at

Gabby. 'Sorry, love,' she said. 'Mum gets a bit confused sometimes. She doesn't mean any harm by it, really.' She took the old lady by the arm and led her away. 'Come on, Mum. Let's go to the OK Café for a cuppa.'

'Ooh, yes,' cooed the old lady. 'That would be lovely!'

Mother and daughter strolled away arm-in-arm, serene. Gabby shook her head slowly. The old lady suddenly looked back at Gabby and thrust a bony little finger in her direction. 'I'm watching you, *thug*!' she rasped. And then they vanished around the corner.

Gabby leaned against the shop door and breathed a colossal sigh. When her temper had subsided and her breathing returned to its normal rate, she peeped around the doorway once more, expecting to find Chas had vanished.

But Chas was still there outside the hi-fi shop, absorbed in his window shopping. After a moment he thrust his hands into his coat pockets and set off up the street. Gabby waited for him to get a safe distance ahead and stepped out of the doorway.

The street was dotted with shoppers trudging along, plastic carrier bags dangling from their hands. Dusk was fast approaching. The colours of the town were draining away to a uniform slate grey. Chas trotted over a zebra crossing, head down, apparently lost in his thoughts. She watched as he rounded the corner into a narrow passageway separating two blocks of shops. Her heart began to beat faster. She knew there was only a high fence at the end of the alley – it was a dead end. Moving quickly, stepping with care to prevent her footsteps from making too much noise, she scurried after him. Pressing herself flat against the wall beside the mouth of the passageway, she peeked around the corner. What she saw made her jaw drop.

CHAPTER FOUR
LIFESKILLZ (WITH A 'Z')

The shoe was full of spoons.

Barney picked them out one by one. *Eight, nine, ten* ... ten spoons. He gathered them together and checked the other shoe. In it he found a single house sparrow. The greyish-brown bird seemed somewhat perplexed and alarmed. With great care, he took the sparrow in one hand, feeling the warmth and fragility of this tiny scrap of life, and opened the hall window, taking care not to knock over a tall plaster statuette of a horse standing on

the windowsill. He tried to imagine what thoughts were running through the sparrow's mind. A shoe is not, by any stretch of the imagination, the natural habitat of a bird, nor is the interior of a human house, even if the bird in question is called a house sparrow. The creature had, he realised, been plunged into a completely alien world. Its senses would be bombarding its mind with questions it was in no position to answer. In other words, it was probably well freaking out. He unclasped his fingers. The sparrow didn't hang about and zoomed straight into the waiting branches of a tall tree in the garden. It looked back at Barney, as if memorising his face in case it was one day called upon to pick him out of a police identity parade.

'What's in there today?' asked Gill, the wheeze in her voice worse than ever, as she watched him from the doorway of the kitchen. She was leaning heavily on her walking frame.

'Ten spoons and a sparrow,' said Barney.

Gill snorted. 'What does my husband think he is? A cat? He'll want you to scratch his ears next. Come through, Barney. The kettle's on.' She turned and headed into the kitchen, moving slowly and with difficulty, the rubber-tipped feet of her creaky walking frame clattering against the tiled floor.

Barney followed.

Dave was sitting hunched over the kitchen table, slowly peeling an apple with great concentration. He became aware of the other two in the kitchen and his eyes flicked upwards. His drooping mouth suddenly formed itself into a big smile. 'Thomas!' he cried happily, then shook his head. 'I mean George! No, Morris! Daniel? Rufus! Martin? ... Ian! Haha! Hello, Ian!'

'It's Barney,' said Barney.

'Barney!' said Dave. 'Of course, young man. Barney! How are you?'

'I'm fine, thanks,' said Barney. 'How are you today, Dave?'

'Splendid!' said Dave, putting down the apple peeler. 'Splendid as ever! Peckish, though. I was going to have some treacle pudding but all the spoons have vanished. Imagine that! Who'd want to steal a lot of spoons? It's quite a mystery.'

Barney showed him the spoons. 'Mystery solved.'

'Good lord!' exclaimed Dave. 'Where did you find those?'

'He saw them sticking out of one of your shoes in the rack by the front door,' said Gill, wearily. She poured hot water from the kettle into the teapot. 'There was a sparrow in the other one. Maybe we should start calling you Tiddles.'

'Really?' said Dave. 'A sparrow? How extraordinary!'

'Not really,' muttered Gill. 'If you'd let Barney put the washing-up away like he's supposed to we wouldn't have these problems. It's like living with a five-year-old child sometimes.' She reached into the pocket of her cardigan and drew out a packet of cigarettes and a lighter. She placed a cigarette between her lips with gnarled fingers and fumbled with the bright red plastic lighter until a small yellow flame appeared. She lit the cigarette and quickly exhaled a cloud of grey smoke. It hung in the air of the kitchen, drifting slowly like ghostly wisps of mist.

Barney wrinkled his nose. Dave and Gill weren't supposed to smoke when he was in the house. It was part of the agreement with the school. But they always did and he could never bring himself to object. They seemed to have such few pleasures in their lives that he felt bad about trying to stop this one, even if it did mean he would be going home with his jumper and hair reeking of smoke again.

He guessed Dave and Gill were in their

seventies. Gill used a walking frame and had a cough that sounded like the dilapidated foot pump that Barney's dad used to inflate the airbed on camping trips. Her long, fine, grey hair was usually tied back in a neat ponytail. Arthritis had begun to clench her limbs into painful and much less useful versions of their former selves. But beneath her thick, owlish glasses she had small, sharp, intelligent eyes that saw everything and Barney sensed that a rather brilliant mind lurked beneath her grumpy-old-lady act. Dave, on the other hand …

… Dave was *lovely*, thought Barney. He was a big, kindly, teddy bear of a man, always the first to laugh at his own deteriorating memory. Garden birds in shoes was nothing. The previous week, Barney had found Dave's wallet in the oven, marinating slowly in a red wine and onion sauce. The week before that, Dave had spent a whole hour planting a fish finger in a flowerpot as if it were a sapling before Barney and Gill realised what he was up to. It was as if the house was plagued by a particularly mischievous poltergeist. He wished Gill could see the funny side of Dave's mistakes as much as Dave himself did, but he could only guess how hard it must be for her to see Dave's mind slowly unravelling before her eyes.

Gill placed three cups of tea on a tray and carried it, rattling and sloshing, towards the table, her legs juddering without the aid of the walking frame.

Barney leaped to his feet. 'Let me get that.'

'Sit down,' snapped Gill, her cigarette clenched between her teeth. 'I'm not a complete invalid.' She lowered the tray on to the table with precise, careful movements and half slid, half collapsed into a chair opposite Dave. She squinted into her saucer. 'More tea in there than the cup,' she wheezed and gave a great laugh.

Barney laughed politely and sipped his tea,

aware of a strange tension suddenly in the atmosphere

'I can predict your future, Rufus!'

'It's Barney,' said Barney quietly. 'And can you?'

'I can predict your future, Barney,' repeated Dave, without missing a beat.

Gill exhaled a blast of smoke upwards. She raised her eyebrows.

Dave held up a hand. Dangling from it was the peel from his apple, removed in a single long coil. He let it bob up and down for a second like some low-rent Slinky. 'I can tell you who you're going to marry.'

Barney felt himself blush. 'That's ridiculous!' he blurted out, somewhat louder than he intended.

'We shall see,' said Dave with a smile. 'Take the peel.' He handed it to Barney. Barney gripped the end between his thumb and forefinger. The green spiral of peel rotated slowly over the tabletop. Gill watched, amused as Dave began to recite in a booming voice:

'Spirits all-knowing,

May thee reveal,

His True Love's Initial,

By the shape of this peel!'

Barney stared at the peel, dumbstruck, as if it might suddenly start to talk or magically transform itself into a pterodactyl.

'You have to drop the peel on to the table, son,' said Dave.

'Oh. Right.' Barney let go of the peel. It flopped on the tabletop. Dave and Gill both leaned in eagerly to peer at it.

Barney's heart turned a somersault. *Don't be G*, he thought. *Don't be G ...*

'G,' said Gill. 'Definitely a G.'

'I agree, dear,' said Dave. 'G it is. Do you know any girls whose name starts with a G, Thomas?'

'My name's Barney,' said Barney, his blood ringing in his ears. 'And ... erm ... maybe. One. Possibly one. Possibly more. I know lots of young ladies. Well, some.' He sensed he needed to shut up as soon as possible.

'Well, there you go,' said Dave. 'She's your future wife. Is it the first or second name that starts with a G?'

'Both actually,' said Barney sheepishly.

Gill nodded sagely. 'You see, Barney. The peel never lies. When are you going to propose to her?' She and Dave looked at him with grave expressions – and suddenly burst into helpless laughter. 'It's only a silly game, my love!' hooted Gill. 'Don't look so worried!'

'The look on your face, Rufus!' said Dave, shaking his head. 'Absolutely priceless!'

'It's Barney!' said Barney, wishing he had skived off LifeSkillz today. 'And I knew you were just joking. Honestly. It was obvious.'

'Yeah, right,' said Gill, still giggling. 'He had you hook, line and sinker.'

'What does it say about young people today if

they're prepared to take relationship advice from a piece of kitchen waste?' said Dave, and that set him and Gill off laughing again.

'I knew you were just joking,' insisted Barney. 'I don't believe in the paranormal. Really. Me and Gab–' He checked himself. '*I* believe there's a rational explanation for everything. There are no spirits. No ghosts.'

'No mysteries in life, eh?' said Dave. His laughter was subsiding now.

'I didn't say that,' said Barney. 'Of course there are still mysteries to investigate, things we don't know.'

'You ever hear about the backwards robot?' said Dave. 'That's a good mystery. A local one.'

'No,' said Barney, interested. 'What is it?'

Gill suddenly emitted a blast of smoke from her nostrils like a dragon. 'Dave's babbling,' she said dismissively. 'Don't listen to him.' She stood up as quickly as she could, pressing down hard on the table to lever herself up. 'Come and give me a hand baking this flan. Can't sit here gossiping all day.'

'I'm not babbling,' said Dave. 'I remember it well–'

'Will you be quiet? Silly old man,' said Gill loudly, her back to him, heading for the kitchen counter. 'Barney doesn't need to hear your nonsense.'

'I don't mind,' said Barney. 'I like stories.'

'Don't encourage him,' she retorted. She suddenly reminded Barney of a very mean maths teacher he had known in primary school. 'You know his mind's not what it once was. The last thing he needs is you humouring his idiocy. I'd like you to leave now, please.'

'What?' said Barney. 'I haven't done anything?'

'Do you want me to get on the phone to your school and tell them you've been upsetting my husband?' said Gill. 'I'll do it if you don't leave right now.'

Barney held up his hands. 'Whoa! I'm going!

Sorry! I didn't mean to ...' He stood up. Dave was staring at him. There was something in his eyes resembling fear. Barney suddenly felt very out of his depth. He headed for the kitchen door. 'Sorry again,' he muttered.

'Just go, Barney,' said Gill, flatly. 'It's not your fault. We'll see you on Thursday.'

Barney let himself out and walked up the driveway. After the smoky interior of Gill and Dave's house, the afternoon air was as cold and refreshing as a glass of milk.

CHAPTER FIVE
FIVE HUNDRED CERAMIC BINTURONGS

'Wow! Big wow! Wowsers!'

'That's exactly what I thought.'

'What, those exact words? In that exact order?'

Gabby rolled her eyes. 'All right. Not *exactly* those words. But what I saw was pretty darn wow-worthy.'

'I bet it was! And you're *positive* it wasn't a trick of some kind?'

Gabby laughed. 'Barney, mate – Chas vanished into thin air. No smoke. No trapdoors. He put his schoolbag down on the ground – just an ordinary sports bag – opened it, and then jumped into it as if it were a hole seven metres deep! He vanished! There was a flash of light and then even the bag was gone. That's exactly what I saw. I promise.'

'There wasn't a hole in the ground?'

'Absolutely not. I checked ten times. Normal paving stones.'

'And you haven't been hypnotised? Or drugged? Or had your brain jiggled with in any way?'

Gabby shrugged. 'If I had I wouldn't know so it's pointless asking, isn't it?'

'Hmm. Good point,' said Barney. He chewed his thumbnail.

They were sitting at the kitchen table in Gabby's house. Two mugs of tea stood in front of them slowly going cold, as neither of them had stopped talking long enough to take a single sip.

It was a very different kitchen to the one Barney had encountered on his first visit to Gabby's house a few months earlier. Back then, the kitchen, and actually every other room in the house, had been covered by a layer of leaves. Gabby's mum had, for complicated reasons of her own, developed an obsession with leaves of all kinds and had taken to attaching them to every square centimetre of space in the house. Thankfully, this phase had run its course and the kitchen now looked perfectly normal. Mrs Grayling herself was pottering about the kitchen, humming softly to herself and paying no attention to Barney and Gabby at all.

Frowning, Gabby cupped her chin in her hand. 'So what are we talking about here? Some kind of Einstein-Rosen Bridge? Is that even physically possible?'

'Well, you might be talking about Einstein-Rosen Bridges,' said Barney, 'but, personally, I haven't got a clue what one is.'

'They're theoretical wormholes in space,' said Gabby as if reminding him of something he had always known.

'Oh, yeah. *Course*,' said Barney. 'Look, Gab.' He pointed to his face. 'Observe. This is what a confused person looks like. Someone who has never heard about Einstein's bungholes.'

'*Wormholes*.'

'Whatever.' A thought suddenly struck Barney. 'Wait a minute – are you *clever*?'

'What?'

'Are you clever, Gab? You know – really intelligent. Brainy. It would explain a lot.'

Gabby shrugged. 'Clever? Well, no, not really. I just read lots of books and remember what they say.'

Barney groaned. 'That's what clever is, you idiot! You are! You're really clever. How did I not know this?'

'Stop saying that,' said Gabby, blushing. 'I'm not especially clever. Honest.'

'Oh, yeah? Do you think many teenage girls know about Einstein-Rosen Dual Carriageways?'

'Bridges. Not dual carriageways. Although it's an intriguing concept.'

'See? That was a clever thing to say. It proves you're clever!'

Gabby chuckled. 'OK, so maybe I am a little bit. But so what?'

'It's just that I've never really known anybody clever before,' said Barney thoughtfully. 'It's really cool. You know about all sorts of stuff. I'd like to be like that one day.'

'Well, thanks, mate,' said Gabby, blushing.

'So what are we going to do about Chas?'

Gabby grinned. 'Same thing Geek Inc. always does when confronted with the impossible. We investigate! Let's keep a close eye on him. See what else he's capable of.'

A serious look appeared on Barney's face. 'Do you think he might be – you know – *dangerous*?'

Gabby frowned and wrinkled her nose. 'He seems like a nice-enough lad. And he's only doing a few tricks, isn't he? *Euch!* This tea's gone cold. Do you want another cup?'

'Sure,' said Barney, handing her his mug.

Gabby emptied away their cold tea and filled the kettle. 'How are you getting on with your old couple, by the way – what are they called again ...?'

'Dave and Gill. Not bad. Gill can be a right moody-chops sometimes. She gets so impatient with Dave losing his memory. Not his fault, poor guy. The other day he starts babbling on about a backwards robot and Gill says–'

Gabby's mum suddenly gave a little squeak. 'Oooh! The backwards robot! That takes me back!'

Barney stared at her. 'You mean it's real? There's an actual backwards robot? I thought it was just some random stuff coming out of Dave's brain.'

'It's real enough,' said Mrs Grayling. 'It's in the park somewhere. Here in Blue Hills. I was there when the mayor unveiled it. It's a statue, you see. Strange business.'

'What's this?' said Gabby, putting down the kettle. 'If it's something strange then Barney and I definitely want to know more.'

'It is a very weird story, now I think about it,' said Mrs Grayling. 'But I'm not the best person to tell it. There's a lady in this street who knows far more about it. She was involved, you see.'

Gabby and Barney exchanged a look of perfect confusion.

Gabby pressed the doorbell. A crude electronic version of 'Three Blind Mice' sounded within the house. It went on for a very long time.

'Haven't we got enough odd stuff on our plate investigating Chas Hinton's magic tricks?' Barney asked.

'We're in the middle of an oddness-drought,' grinned Gabby. 'I'm not missing the opportunity to look into something else weird. And I'm sure Sherlock Holmes wouldn't turn his nose up at a mystery like this.'

Barney flushed with colour. 'You must have thought I was an idiot talking about him the other day.'

Gabby laughed. 'No worries, Barney. Easy mistake to make.'

'No, I should have realised he died after that battle with Professor Moriarty at the Reichenbach Falls. I feel such a fool.'

Gabby made the snorting sound again.

'Hay fever again?'

'Yeah. Can't seem to shake it,' she said, suppressing a grin.

The door opened and a tall, brittle-looking woman in her late fifties stood in front of them. Her face was etched with deep lines and her hair was cut in a weird asymmetrical style. A pair of large fish-shaped earrings danced and jerked against her neck, almost as if they were live fish struggling on hooks.

'Fiona Cress?' asked Gabby.

'Oh excellent! You're here!' the woman exclaimed. 'Come this way! The binturongs are waiting.'

Hundreds of pairs of tiny eyes stared down at Gabby and Barney from rows of wooden shelves lining the room. The eyes belonged to hundreds of small glazed pottery creatures. Barney couldn't tell if they were meant to be cats, or dogs or bears – or what. What he did know was that their weird, whiskery little faces were starting to seriously freak him out. It felt like they might suddenly come alive, pounce down from their shelves and devour them.

'Welcome to my studio,' said Fiona Cress.

'Would you like tea? Or do you want to get started moving the binturongs right away?'

Barney looked at Gabby. 'Once again, if you want to know what a totally confused person looks like, just take a look at me,' he muttered.

Gabby gave Fiona Cress her politest smile. 'I'm afraid there's been a mistake. We're not here about the binturongs.'

'What?' Fiona Cress's eyebrows narrowed. 'You've not come to take them away?'

'No,' said Gabby. 'We haven't.'

'What *are* binturongs?' said Barney, feeling faintly embarrassed, as if he might have just accidentally sworn in a foreign language.

'Binturongs,' explained Gabby hurriedly, 'are a nocturnal mammal native to East Asia. They live in trees and smell of popcorn.'

'You're making this up,' said Barney. 'There's no such thing.'

'No such thing?' hooted Fiona Cress. Her voice

sounded so alarmed that Barney actually jumped. 'What on Earth are they teaching you kids in schools these days?'

Barney shrugged. 'I dunno. Maths and stuff. Not about weird animals. It doesn't tend to help with college applications.'

Fiona Cress waved a hand at the rows of pottery creatures. Chunky bangles rattled on her wrist. 'Binturongs are beautiful, amiable creatures of the forest canopy, much loved by the Orang Asli people of Malaysia. And I've just made five hundred of them in ceramic. Had a big order from a chain of Malaysian restaurants. I take it you're not here to collect them, then?'

'No,' said Barney, eager to move the conversation away from binturongs. 'We came here to ask you something.'

Fiona Cress narrowed her eyes. 'Oh really? What do you want? I'm a busy woman.'

'We want to know about the backwards robot,'

said Gabby. 'We understand you had something to do with it.'

The lines on Fiona Cress's face momentarily vanished as a look of astonishment swept over her features. 'The *robot*? Good lord. I've haven't thought about all that business in decades. Who are you anyway? Why do you want to know about it?'

'It was odd, apparently,' said Barney. 'And we like things that are odd. Can you tell us about it?'

Fiona Cress lifted a long, oddly-striped, fur coat off a nearby peg and slipped it on. Barney wondered what obscure creatures had contributed to its manufacture.

'I can do better than that,' she said. 'Come on.'

The park was silent and still in the twilight. Fiona marched towards some distant trees, her long coat flapping behind her. Gabby and Barney followed, struggling to keep up.She seemed to have very long legs and a stride like a giraffe's.

'You have to appreciate,' Fiona was saying, 'it all happened a very long time ago. Thirty – forty years, for heaven's sake. So forgive me if my memory is a little dimmed by the ravages of time. They were opening a new playground here in the park – slides, roundabouts, you get the picture. And the mayor – a frightful bore of a man – asked me to produce a statue to commemorate the opening. Seems some TV company had told him they'd pay for it as long as the statue promoted one of their kids' programmes. It was a show called *The Robin and the Robot*. Did you ever see it?'

Gabby shook her head. 'Umm, probably a bit before our time.'

Fiona smiled politely. 'Of course, darling. Ah. Here, look.'

They had arrived at a tall clump of youngish trees and bushes.

'What are we looking at?' asked Gabby cautiously. She was suddenly aware that she had let this strange woman lead her and Barney into a dark and isolated corner of the park just as night was falling. Everything she'd ever been told about stranger danger was now flashing through her mind.

'The mayor was going to fence this area off, but rather than pay for a fence to be built he just moved a load of bushes and trees to hide it,' said Fiona. 'What you want is through here. Follow me.' She advanced into the undergrowth, pushing her way through the bushes, her striped fur coat disappearing amidst the tangle of stems and branches.

Barney stood aside, gesturing for Gabby to go first. 'Ladies first.'

'Cheers,' muttered Gabby. She pulled the zip of her parka up to her chin and strode into the dark bushes, arms raised to protect her face from the sharp branches. Barney followed closely behind.

Suddenly feeling concrete underfoot, they

emerged into a small circular clearing. Fiona was standing at its centre, arms folded, wearing a strange, faraway expression. Around her they saw a child's slide made of stained and tarnished metal, a small roundabout covered in flaking paint, and a sorry-looking swing hanging lopsidedly from a single rusty chain. The bases of all three were choked with thick tufts of long weeds that had sprouted through cracks in the concrete. Fiona was gesturing towards a fourth object in the clearing.

'There she is. Or rather *they are*. Mustn't forget Bobby Robin, must we?'

Barney and Gabby saw a smallish granite statue – a chipped and rain-dirtied thing, its base also obscured by weeds. It depicted a weird human-shaped robot in a long coat and hat standing with its foot on a large rectangular sign, one hand raised in a friendly wave. On the other hand, like something from a Christmas card, sat a fat little robin, the end of its tail apparently long since snapped off and lost. There was something almost overpoweringly sad about the statue, it seemed to Barney, as if the two characters had come to this clearing many years ago during some game of hide-and-seek and were still waiting patiently to be discovered.

Gabby knelt down in front of the statue to inspect the words inscribed into the sign. With the sleeve of her coat she wiped away some dried mud.

'It says "The Robin and the Robot". But the writing's backwards.'

'The whole thing's backwards,' said Fiona. 'When I carved the statue the robot Cluedroid was holding Bobby Robin in its left hand. Now he's in its right.'

'So how did it get reversed?'

'No one knows,' said Fiona Cress. 'There was some odd gas explosion when the statue was unveiled, but there's no way an explosion can turn something into a mirror image of itself, is there? I thought maybe I was going mad and had carved it backwards all along and maybe I was seeing everything reversed. But when I saw some photos I'd taken of the half-completed statue it proved the writing had been the correct way around when I was making it.'

Gabby ran her finger along the backwards words on the sign. 'Wowsers,' she said softly. 'That's a real mystery.'

'No one cares about it, though,' said Fiona, a tired and sombre note in her voice. 'A young girl went missing at the time the statue was unveiled. Terrible business – and a much more important mystery than some silly statue. It was in all the papers for a while. She never was found and nobody wanted to use this playground after that. It was awful – poor little Fleur Abbott. Her parents still live in Blue Hills. I see them in the street sometimes. You can see in their faces the sadness has never left them.'

Barney gave a sudden gasp. He turned to Fiona. 'Did you say her name was Fleur *Abbott*?'

'Yes,' said Fiona Cress. 'Why?'

'Do you know what her parents are called?'

'I do. They're called—'

'*Dave and Gill*,' Barney finished for her. 'They're called Dave and Gill, aren't they?'

Fiona Cress nodded. The wooden fish on her earrings danced and swayed like hanged men.

CHAPTER SIX
THE SOCIETY OF HIGHLY UNUSUAL THINGS

Gabby lay in bed, somewhere between sleep and waking, weird chains of thoughts streaming and tumbling through her mind. Outside, she could hear the fractured music of the dawn chorus. Around her the duvet felt soft and enveloping as steam, her limbs as heavy as stone.

She thought about Chas Hinton, how he had impossibly jumped inside his own schoolbag and vanished. She thought of the doves soaring out of the paper bag, of Barney's EGG dropping into his waiting hands, and of the look of amazement and joy on her friend's face at having his game returned to him.

Last night Gabby had posted a message on an Internet forum she sometimes frequented, a place where school kids swapped advice and tried to help with one another's problems. She uploaded a photo of Chas that Laura had taken with her mobile phone and asked if anyone knew of this strange kid and his magical gifts. Maybe someone out there might have a little information about him. He had to have come from somewhere. In the photo Chas had been wearing a small, knowing smile, making him look a bit like a male Mona Lisa. Chas's smile now swam before her mind's eye, Cheshire Cat-like, hinting at some strange and incredible secret.

Next she thought about Fiona Cress and her weird army of pottery binturongs, of the chill that had entered the woman's voice when she talked of the missing girl, Fleur Abbott, and of the look of astonishment on Barney's face when he realised the elderly couple he had been visiting must be Fleur's parents.

Thinking about the missing girl brought Gabby's thoughts round to her dad. It was six months since he had vanished without a single word to her or her mother. The Ministry of Defence where he worked had offered no clue to his whereabouts. Neither had the Blue Hills police, who seemed at a loss as to how to track him down.Some time ago she had realised that her best bet for finding her father would be her own investigations, but so far she had found out nothing. She thought of a man called Orville McIntyre, a colleague of her dad's with whom she and Barney had dealt during that strange business with Gloria Pickles last year. He had been extremely friendly and helpful at first but then revealed a somewhat darker, more ruthless side to his character when events had turned serious. In a far corner of her mind, a vague suspicion nagged that he knew more about her dad's disappearance than he was letting on.

An image of the statue in the park now appeared in her mind. In the vision, the robin and the robot came alive, the rain-streaked mottled granite turning to vibrant living colours, the robot's face a gleaming silver, the robin's breast a vivid orange-red. The little bird fluttered off the robot's palm and seemed to alight on Gabby's shoulder. It pressed its tiny beak to her ear.

'It's OK, Gab,' it whispered, 'we're here now.'

Before she could ponder this statement, a shrill buzzing noise obliterated all thoughts from her mind. With a jolt, her eyes snapped open. Thin streaks of dim morning light were piercing the cracks in her curtains, crisscrossing her duvet with silvery lines. She rolled over and clapped a hand to the snooze button of her clock radio. The buzzing noise ceased. She scooped her glasses and mobile phone off the bedside table and settled comfortably back against her pillows. Thumbs working busily, she used her phone to log on to the advice forum, hoping someone had replied to her request for info on Chas.

She gave a soft squeal of surprise.

RE: DO YOU KNOW THIS BOY? 329 REPLIES

Yes, I know him! He's just started at our school, Beaverbrook Comprehensive in Tattenhall. He's a bit of a freak to be honest! He does these weird magic tricks ...

I kno this boi. He is called Charles Hinton and gos too Orange Tree Grammar. He is very wierd ...

The kid in your photo has recently enrolled at the King's School, Chester. He appears to be a talented conjuror who enjoys ...

Gabby scrolled down the list of responses, slowly shaking her head. There were over three hundred sightings of Chas from kids all over the

British Isles – all saying he had just started at their own schools. This was *properly*, *impossibly* weird. How on earth could one boy simultaneously attend all these different schools?

Crazy theories began to jostle for position in Gabby's mind. First, that the multiple Chases were alien invaders who had copied the appearance of a single Earth boy to blend into human society. Then, they were all in fact the same person – a boy who could move impossibly quickly and attend three hundred and twenty-nine different schools on the same day. Then they were actually an army of clones bred by the government for – what, though? Magic tricks? She giggled. Whatever the explanation for this was, she couldn't wait to start investigating.

Barney's arms were on fire.

That's what it felt like, anyway. Never had he experienced pain so acute and so all-encompassing. His legs didn't seem to be in much better condition, either. Or his back. He placed the cardboard box down on the musty bed and sat down beside it, panting like a dog on a hot day. With the back of his hand, he wiped a thick smear of sweat from his forehead.

He looked at his watch. One forty-five. He had only been shifting boxes for fifteen minutes. He heaved a long, hissing sigh. Were they trying to kill him?

When he arrived at the Abbotts' house that afternoon he had been worried that Gill would be in the same foul mood that he had left her in at the end of his last visit. But today she was cheerful, greeting him like a favourite grandson. Dave was having a check-up at the local hospital today and in his absence Gill had made a long list of chores for Barney to do. The first item on it was to move a number of cardboard boxes out of their spare room and empty the contents into the various recycling bins in the garden.

The boxes were so heavy and awkward that at first he thought they must contain old engine parts or bathroom tiles. But when he opened the first box at the bottom of the Abbotts' garden he realised it was filled with nothing heavier than bits of old paper. He was stunned at how heavy a box filled with paper could actually be. Awarding himself a five-minute break, Barney idly prised open the flaps of the cardboard box sitting next to him and drew out the top sheet of paper. It was dog-eared and thinning with age almost to the point of translucency. The words on it had been neatly and densely typed on an old-fashioned typewriter.

```
FRIDAY 6th AUGUST 1976 (CONT'D)
     eventually found one of the type
described by Roderick Branwen in a
junk shop in Kings Street, Mold,
North Wales. The locket is
inscribed with pictures of angels
```

and so far proving as hard to open
as any found by Branwen himself.
There appears to be some secret to
the locking mechanism, almost
certainly some quite simple trick,
which I have not yet been able to
fathom. I am convinced that if I
work at this problem for a few more
hours I shall have discovered its

Barney put the page aside and drew out a handful
more. One had wider line spacing, making it easier
to read, and appeared to be the title page of a
document. It read:

THE SOCIETY OF HIGHLY UNUSUAL THINGS
    AGENDA FOR MEETING — MAY 1976
1) Minutes of previous meeting
2) St Martin's Church poltergeist
3) Invisible milkman?

4) Microscopic dragons

5) Time-travelling tourist in Boots
   the Chemist

6) Yeti sighting in Derbyshire
   Peaks

7) DJ on Blue Hills FM is
   reincarnation of Sir Isaac
   Newton

8) Can herons predict the stock
   market?

Barney stifled a gasp. He reached into the box and pulled out a thick sheaf of paper. Taking a sheet at random from the middle of the pile he studied it, his mouth slowly sagging open in surprise.

13th FEBRUARY 1971 (CONT'D)
   seems likely the creature
menacing the Thompsons' gift shop
is indeed a cockatrice. The tracks

are definitely those of a two-
legged creature and the presence of
chicken feathers confirm

'I thought I told you to throw those away.'

Gill's voice cut through Barney like a sword.

'I'm – I'm sorry,' he stammered, heart pounding. 'I was just taking a break. My arms are tired.' He clambered off the bed hurriedly.

Gill took the sheet of paper from his hand and squinted at it. She snorted and crumpled it in her wrinkled fist. 'Should have thrown out this rubbish a long time ago.' She tossed the ball of paper into the cardboard box.

'What's the Society of Highly Unusual Things?' asked Barney.

'Nothing to concern you,' said Gill. 'A lot of nonsense from a very long time ago, that's all. Now come on, there's plenty more of these boxes to shift.'

'Did you investigate weird things that happened in Blue Hills? Is that what the society did?'

'Forget it,' snapped Gill. All friendliness had drained from her voice. 'I don't want to talk about it. Now move. Work to do.'

'It's just that me and my friend Gabby do exactly the same thing!' Barney pressed on excitedly. 'We have a club called Geek Inc. We love investigating strange happenings. Are all the things written down here true? Can I show the papers to Gabby? She'd love to see them.'

'No. Just throw everything out.' Gill turned her back to him, the walker rattling in her hands. 'Can't have this old junk cluttering up the house.'

'We spoke to Fiona Cress,' said Barney. 'She told us about the backwards robot. And about ... Fleur. Was that why you started investigating strange occurrences?'

Gill's legs suddenly buckled and she clutched at her walking frame for support, her whole body trembling. Barney rushed to help her. Her mouth had puckered into a grimace and big shiny tears began to form at the corners of her eyes.In that instant Barney thought she looked more like a little girl than a woman in her seventies.

'Gill? Are you OK? Come and sit down.' He led her quickly to the bed and sat her down.

'Leave me alone.' Gill pushed him away. She was surprisingly strong. 'Why did you speak to that woman?' she sobbed. 'Why would you want to drag up all that pain from so long ago?'

'I'm so sorry,' said Barney. 'We just like finding out things, that's all. It was curiosity.'

'Curiosity!' spat Gill. 'That's what tore our lives apart. Our own stupid, selfish curiosity. We loved mysteries. Highly unusual things, we called them. Loved investigating them. Fancied ourselves as a right little Holmes-and-Watson team. So many weird things in this town to investigate too. It's like a toyshop for the curious. We had a fine old time.

Well, I'll tell you, Barney – it was our curiosity that cost us our daughter. I think I *unleashed* something that afternoon in 1976 – some force. And it took Fleur from us. It's the only explanation that makes sense. There was only one mystery in our lives from then on. How to live without our daughter. And no number of cockatrices or invisible men was ever going to hold our interest for a second after that. We gave up our investigations.'

Barney spoke softly. 'But didn't you want to investigate what happened to Fleur?'

She looked him in the eye. 'It was our dabblings that lost us our daughter, Barney. I was determined that whatever took her away wouldn't happen again and take someone else's child. We'd discovered some miraculous, mind-blowing things, but in the end I decided the best thing was to shut the society down. Curiosity was just too expensive a pastime.'

'What about Dave?'

'What about him?'

'The stuff in these boxes. They're his memories, too.'

Gill rose slowly and painfully to her feet, knuckles whitening as she gripped her walking frame. 'I don't know whether you've noticed, Barney,' she said quietly, 'but my husband has no use for memories any more.' She shuffled out of the room, the walking frame squeaking and rattling, and closed the door behind her.

CHAPTER SEVEN
A GAME OF CONKERS

Gabby stepped down from the bus and watched as it chugged away along the narrow tree-lined lane. It was a bright afternoon and the sky above was a flawless blue canopy. Not far away a pair of blackbirds darted among the sun-dappled branches, orange beaks and eyes flashing. A tiny russet face poked out of a nearby hedge and regarded her. She winked at it. The weasel returned her gaze fiercely for a moment and then scurried back into the undergrowth.

Gabby smiled. She was starting to see the attraction of skipping school.

Thrusting her hands into the pockets of her parka, she set off up the lane at a leisurely pace, humming a tune to herself. It was good to feel the reassuring thickness of her notebook in her pocket. Making notes about stuff always made her feel more in control of any situation, like she was a proper investigator.

The great part about being a trustworthy, reliable pupil, thought Gabby – one who always did her homework on time, was never told off for talking in class, never late – was that whenever she *did* stray from the straight and narrow, she was never suspected. Teachers never checked up on her excuses, never doubted whether the signature on a permission slip was really her mother's, or, as in this case, never even guessed that the appointment card for a check-up at Blue Hills Cottage Hospital this afternoon had actually been designed and printed off on her own computer that morning. If you behaved yourself most of the time you could get away with so much more than if you were always on the teachers' radars. The trick, of course, was to choose your moments and not do it too often.

Woodlark Grove High School lay at the end of the lane. Gabby had chosen it because it was only a few miles from Blue Hills and relatively small for a comprehensive. Even so, it would be hard enough to spot a single boy among the mass of children that would soon surge through the school's front gate. There was an old-fashioned red telephone box on the opposite side of the street to the school. It stood next to a few horse chestnut trees and beside some steps leading down to a canalside. Gabby decided the phone box would make a good hiding place to watch from. She swung open its heavy iron-framed door and slipped inside. The air within was still and silent and Gabby suddenly became very aware of the sound of her own breathing. On a whim, she breathed a patch of hot, grey-white condensation on to the windowpane in front of her face and dabbed a smiley face into it with the tip of her forefinger.

From the other side of the glass, two real eyes appeared through the eyes of the smiley face. Gabby stepped back, knocking the telephone receiver off its cradle. She pushed open the door of the kiosk.

'Gabby! Hello!'

He was wearing a different school uniform, but otherwise it was him. Chas ran his long fingers through the flick of blond hair covering his forehead.

'Chas! Where did you suddenly appear from?'

The boy laughed heartily. 'Well! That is the question, really, isn't it?'

'You're not the Chas I know from Blue Hills High,

are you?' said Gabby, studying him. 'You're another one. A duplicate, absolutely identical. So what are you, then? A clone? A shapeshifter? A bunch of creatures from Mars disguised as the same human being?'

'Blimey,' said Chas. 'You don't hang about, do you? Straight in there with the big questions.'

'Are you going to tell me?'

'Maybe,' said Chas with a grin. 'If your mind can comprehend the staggering truth.'

Gabby snorted. 'Don't you worry about me. My mind can comprehend some pretty weird stuff, even if I do say so myself.'

'It's a lovely afternoon,' said Chas. 'Shall we take a stroll? Before the school empties out and everywhere's overrun with kids.' He held out his arm.

A cold breeze suddenly made the hairs on the back of Gabby's neck prickle. She zipped up her parka, eyeing him uncertainly. 'OK. But you won't disintegrate me or suck my blood or anything?'

Chas shook his head. 'Wasn't really planning to, no.'

'Good,' said Gabby, taking his arm. 'I think it's always better to check these things first.'

They went down the steps and ambled along the canalside. Before either of them could say a word a streak of bright blue light whizzed past Gabby's head.

'Did you see that?' she exclaimed delightedly. 'A kingfisher!'

'Look,' said Chas, pointing. 'It's landed on the ground on the opposite side of the canal. By that old bench. You see it?'

Gabby shaded her eyes and screwed up her face. 'Not really.'

'Here,' said Chas, passing her a chunky pair of binoculars. 'Use these.'

'Great. Thanks.' Gabby took the binoculars and raised them to her eyes. 'I can see it!' she cried. 'It's got a little fish in its beak! Here – you see ...'

She passed back the binoculars. Chas used them to locate the tiny blue-and-orange bird. 'Oh yes!' He was grinning with pleasure.

'There's just one thing I don't understand,' said Gabby.

'What's that? Ooooh – he's off. There he goes.' He lowered the binoculars. 'What don't you understand?'

'Where the heck did you get those binoculars from? You weren't carrying them and you haven't got a bag.'

Chas pointed a finger at her. 'You're good. You notice stuff. No one notices stuff. Even when I parade weirdness in front of them. But you do. You're pretty unique, Gabby.'

Don't you dare blush, Gabby thought to herself. *Just be cool about this*. 'Am I?' she blurted out, her face turning bright red. 'Oh wowsers! Haha! Maybe I am. I dunno. Haha!'

Oh well done, Gab, she thought.

'Well, there are versions of me attending over two thousand schools in this country,' said Chas. 'Two thousand Chases out there all doing impossible things. And you're the only person to realise it. That's some brain you've got.'

She clenched her fists in her coat pocket, willing herself not to blush again. 'But how is that even possible?' she asked. Something felt wrong. 'Oh *great*,' she muttered, suddenly clapping a hand to her forehead. 'Must have left my notebook in the phone kiosk.'

'Not a problem,' said Chas with a strange smile. 'Try your pocket now.'

Gabby slid her hand back into the pocket of her parka. 'It's there!' she gasped. 'My notebook! How? How did you do that? Was it there all the time and you just monkeyed with my brain so I thought it wasn't? Or are you feeding me illusions now?' She whipped the notebook out of her pocket and showed it to him, the pages flapping in the wind.

'Is this really my notebook or just a figment of my imagination?'

Chas laughed. 'It's definitely real, Gabby.'

'So how did you do it? Is it something to do with that sports bag you disappeared into the other night? I followed you, you know.'

'I know. And it didn't take impossible powers to overhear you having an argument with that old lady.'

Gabby snorted. 'Typical Geek Inc. investigation! Complete foul-up! That's the organisation I belong to, by the way. Geek Inc. We investigate impossible things. Like you.'

'That I didn't know,' said Chas. 'Sounds impressive. What other strange phenomena have you looked into?'

Gabby smiled and wagged a finger at him. 'Don't change the subject! One impossible thing at a time. How did you do the bag trick? Anything to do with wormholes in space?'

'Possibly.'

'Teleportation? That would explain how you make things appear and disappear, including yourself.'

'Maybe.

'Is this connected with time at all? Are you able to freeze time? Is that it?'

'Yes and no.'

'Oh come on now.' Gabby halted and stuck a hand on her hip. 'Enough of the cryptic stuff. Please. If you're going to tell me the truth, just tell me. I can take it. I promise. If you don't want to tell me, fine. There's a bus due in four minutes and I can be home in time for my dinner.'

Charles shrugged. 'OK. I'm a hyperbeing from the fourth dimension.'

Gabby opened her mouth but nothing came out. She tried a second time but her jaw just wobbled like a newborn foal taking its first steps. 'You're ... whhhhaaaaat?' she managed eventually.

'Close your mouth, Gabby,' whispered Chas. 'Standing there with it hanging open is not a good look. You'll get drool on your parka.'

'What? Oh, sorry.' Gabby blinked and shook herself. Her face was pale. 'You just told me something very extraordinary, didn't you? And I don't mean about the mouth-open look not being a good one for me. I knew that already. People say it to me all the time. You'd think I'd have learned by now. Now I'm gabbling. Gabbling Gabby, that's me. Sorry. I'll stop talking in a second. I think I'm in shock. I feel a little bit sick. Do you mind if we sit down on this bench?'

'Sure. Let's sit.'

They sat down. Gabby smiled weakly. She was aching and tingling all over. Her palms felt cold and clammy. 'I'm not actually handling this all that well, am I?' she admitted. 'I'm struggling to get my head around what you've just told me. Can you explain it again in slightly simpler terms? I can deal with it,

I promise. It might just take a few moments for all the cogs in my brain to mesh successfully.'

Chas took a deep breath. He placed his hands behind his head and stretched his long legs comfortably. 'I come from a different universe, a place you would call the fourth dimension. All the different copies of me around Britain are actually all parts of the same being. Do you understand?'

'Umm ... not really. Parts of the same being? But how?'

Chas considered for a moment. 'Look down at the canal.'

Gabby leaned forward and stared at the smooth glassy surface of the water. 'I'm looking. Go on.'

'Imagine you're a fish living in the canal – a stickleback, say.'

'OK,' said Gabby. 'Stickleback. Good.'

'To you, Mrs Stickleback, the canal is your entire universe. You have no idea that there is a whole world above the surface of the water. You don't even think of the water as *having* a surface, an edge. To you it's just all there is.'

'Right. With you so far.'

'Now,' said Chas, 'a person comes along – me, for instance. I stick my fingers through the surface of the water – into the stickleback's world. What do you see, Mrs Stickleback?'

'Your hand?'

Chas held up a hand. 'No. What a stickleback would see would be *five worms*.' He wriggled his long fingers, wormlike. 'The stickleback doesn't know the five fingers are all connected to the same hand. It just sees five worms entering its world at five different places.'

Gabby nodded slowly. 'Gotcha.'

'So it's the same with me. All the different copies of me are like the fingers of an enormous hand poking into your world from a higher dimension. All the Chases are really parts of the same large creature.'

'So you're just a finger?'

Chas laughed. 'Yes, I suppose I am.'

'So, why do you look like a person?'

'If you wanted a stickleback to think your finger really was a worm you might paint your finger to look more like one. Same kind of thing with me. I'm in disguise.'

'You're a painted worm? Is that what you're telling me?'

He laughed again.

'So, if all those hundreds and hundreds of copies of you are just parts of the same organism, your true self – how big are you really?'

Chas whistled. 'Pretty darn big, actually. It might seriously blow your mind if I told you.'

Gabby snorted. 'Like it could get much more blown. Go on, tell me.'

He smiled. 'My actual four-dimensional body is roughly twice the size of your solar system.'

Gabby swore. Loudly. She clapped a hand over

her mouth and shut her eyes. 'Sorry!' she mumbled through her hand.

Chas chuckled. 'No problem. I think you're coping pretty well, all things considered. Is the truth starting to sink in yet?'

Gabby shrugged. 'I think so. I guess this would explain the tricks you can do. You reach through this fourth dimension and invisibly grab stuff or put stuff into it to make it disappear.' She rubbed her eyes. 'Cor. I think my brain needs an oil change.'

'There's no such thing as a locked door to me,' said Chas. 'I can see inside everything, reach inside anything. Because your human senses can't detect the fourth dimension, you don't realise that even a locked safe is open to me.' He stood up and plucked a conker from a horse chestnut tree overhanging the bench. He showed its spiky case to Gabby, holding it delicately between thumb and forefinger.

'Watch.'

In a single swift movement, he tapped the conker case with the forefinger of his other hand. A shiny brown conker dropped out. Gabby caught it. Chas handed her the case. It was completely unbroken. 'Open it,' he said.

Taking care not to spike herself, Gabby prised open the conker case. Its soft white interior was completely empty. 'Wowsers,' she muttered softly. 'Is there anything you can't do?'

Chas nodded grimly. 'Yes. I can't go home. You see, I'm stuck in your world. Trapped, like a man with his hand caught in some railings.'

'But you're as big as a solar system,' said Gabby. 'How can a solar system get its hand trapped in some railings?'

'There was an accident,' said Chas. 'I was studying your universe – you three-dimensional beings are fascinating – and part of me, the part you humans now interpret as two thousand copies of the same boy, got . . . well – *wedged* is the best word. I got wedged into your universe. And now I can't get out. It's kind of embarrassing. Bits of me can dip in and out of the fourth dimension to do silly tricks, but some part of me must always remain in your world.'

'But what about your friends, your family, in your universe? Can't they help?'

Chas shook his head. 'No one knows I'm here. And it could be a long time before anyone notices I'm missing. Time works differently in the fourth dimension. It goes in all kinds of weird directions, not just forward like it does here. Your whole universe might end before I'm rescued. I hate to think what might happen to me then.'

'Is there anything you can do?'

'There is,' he said, looking away. He ran a hand through his hair. 'But I'd need some help and it might be dangerous. Could be *very* danger–'

'I'll help.' Gabby spoke automatically. 'Of course I'll help. Why wouldn't I?' Her head was suddenly spinning with delight, her mind racing with countless wild ideas, her heart thudding with joy. *This boy*, she thought, *is capable of anything. Literally anything!*

'You will?' Chas's big blue eyes were wide. 'Really?'

'Really. It's not every day you get to help a boy from another universe, is it? What do I have to do?'

Chas laughed with relief and pleasure. 'Oh, Gabby! You don't know how happy that makes me! You're saving my life. I'll explain the plan later. I have an escape plan, you see, as every self-respecting prisoner ought to. But first ...' He grinned wickedly.

'What?'

'Have you ever been to the fourth dimension?'

Gabby laughed. 'Oh, yeah. All the time. Mum and I have a holiday cottage there. What do you think, you lunatic? Of course not.'

'Fancy a little trip? You'd be the first being from your entire universe to enter it. But it might be a *little* overwhelming at first.'

Gabby squealed. 'Oh wow! That would be incredible!'

They stood up. Chas took Gabby's hand. 'For a three-dimensional girl, you're pretty cool, you know that?'

Before Gabby could reply there was a flash of brilliant white light and they were gone.

CHAPTER EIGHT
ALARMING ACID, BUSHWHACKED BULLIES, HAUNTED HIGHLIGHTERS AND TRASHED TROPHIES

When Barney went to room U13 the next day for Geek Inc., there was no sign of Gabby. He waited patiently for the whole of lunch break, his stomach rumbling fiercely, but still she failed to appear. He guessed she must be ill and made a mental note to text her that night when he got home after football practice. With just a couple of minutes to go before afternoon registration, he dashed to the tuck shop and bought an apple, taking huge wet bites from it as he hurried to his form room.

Pulling open the door at the school's main entrance, he was almost knocked to the ground by the tall, bustling figure of the chemistry teacher, Miss Roberts, who was bursting out of the building in a state of some distress, her high-heeled boots making loud clumping sounds and her dark hair streaming behind her in messy tangles.

'Why don't you look where you're going, you little fool?' she called to him over her shoulder in her sing-song Welsh accent and strode towards the car park.

Barney blinked at her in surprise and went inside.

Clomp-clomp-clomp went Miss Roberts's boots on the tarmac. *What a morning!* she thought. It had all been too much. She needed to go home and unwind on the sofa with box of chocolates and her cat, Captain Fluffmeister, on her lap – and had just informed the headmaster that that was precisely what she was going to do. The headmaster, Mr Siskin, could only nod dumbly – like everyone else in the school he was a bit afraid of Miss Roberts and didn't like disagreeing with her.

She hadn't been looking forward to this morning. She was due to teach a Year Ten class that included that insufferable know-it-all, Gabrielle Grayling. It was obvious that the Grayling girl knew just as much about chemistry as she did herself – if not more – but the thing that really got up Miss Roberts's nose was that Gabby was so unfailingly *nice* the whole time. When a pupil was as bright and gifted as Gabrielle Grayling, you wanted them to have a horrible personality so you didn't feel so bad about hating them. But Gabby was just so quiet and patient and thoughtful that it made her want to scream. On several occasions she had made fun of Gabby in front of the class, banged her metre-long wooden ruler on the desk to startle her, and deliberately given her poorer marks than she deserved, just to see if she could provoke Gabby into some angry reaction, but all her attempts had failed. When Gabby had been absent from this morning's lesson, Miss Roberts had felt a wave of relief.

But as it turned out the lesson had been the most troubling one she had ever taken.

She had been about to demonstrate to the class how mixing zinc with hydrochloric acid produces hydrogen gas, and had the necessary apparatus set up on her desk. In her handbag under the table, her mobile phone suddenly emitted an electronic bleep. She was meant to have her phone switched off in class but she had been waiting all day for a text from her best friend about whether she'd been able to buy tickets to a concert by their favourite boyband. Eagerly, she ducked under her desk. A strange acrid smell greeted her. It was coming from her handbag. She scooped it up and laid it on the desk. Thick, stinking fumes were rising from its interior. Someone had poured acid into it! Everything inside was churning and dissolving as the hissing acid devoured it. She watched, goggle-eyed, as her mobile phone disintegrated into a pool of bubbling plastic and metal.

'WHO DID THIS?' she demanded in a voice that sent icicles of terror through the hearts of her class. 'WHO. IS. RESPONSIBLE?'

The horror-struck Year Ten class stared back, mute with fear. Miss Roberts met their gaze, her eyes narrowing with suspicion. She could normally sniff out a culprit easily, few children being able to withstand her ferocious stare, but today all the kids in her chemistry lesson looked equally shocked and alarmed by what had happened.

Very well, she thought. *Time to turn up the pressure*. She'd have the guilty party tearfully confessing in no time. She reached for her metre ruler, which leaned in its usual position against her whiteboard. One swift slap of the ruler on the desk produced a clap as loud as thunder and was usually excellent for inspiring terror in wayward children. But as she raised the ruler to strike it on her desk, its wooden length crumbled to dust in her hands, spraying her with tiny splinters. Someone had dipped it in acid! The fragments of wood clattered softly on to her desk. The class gasped in unison. It was then that Miss Roberts gave up and decided she'd rather be elsewhere. She snatched her coat off the back off her chair. Its collar came away in her hand – the rest of the coat, she saw with horror, reduced to acid-ravaged scraps of cloth. She let out a grunt of frustration and stormed from the class and up the corridor towards the staffroom, where she was pretty sure

Mr Osborn kept a bottle of whisky hidden in the umbrella stand.

This was not the only odd event to happen in Blue Hills High that day. At morning break, a Year Eleven girl named Maisy Quench had been demanding to be given the lunch money of two Year Eight girls. Maisy was explaining that if the two girls didn't hand over their cash, she would push both of their heads down a toilet and flush it, much as she had done to some speccy Year Ten girl called Gabby something the previous week. The two girls exchanged a frightened glance and reached in their schoolbags for their money. But when they looked up, much to their astonishment and relief, Maisy had vanished. She was discovered later that afternoon by a bemused Year Nine girl, her head wedged in a toilet bowl and with no memory of how she had got there. A plumber had to be called to release her.

Another strange occurrence was what happened

to David Brume. David – an eccentric kid whose chief delight in life was scribbling on people's books, clothes and schoolbags with a large fluorescent yellow highlighter pen he called Excalibur – was lurking in a quiet corner of the playground like a spider in its web, waiting for some unsuspecting victim to come within highlighting range. He chuckled quietly to himself as he remembered how the previous week he had drawn a beautiful long yellow line down the back of Gabrielle Grayling's white blouse. Without warning, the highlighter pen jerked out of his hand and pressed its wedge-shaped tip against David's forehead.

'Excalibur,' cried David, 'what's got into you?' He always spoke to his highlighter pen as if it were alive but it had never until this day done anything to suggest it actually was. The pen danced in the air before his eyes and drew another line, this time down his right cheek. He pressed his hand to it. 'Stop it!' he demanded. 'Stop it at once!'

But Excalibur had only just begun.

A few minutes later, a strange bedraggled figure limped into the school nurse's office. Upon seeing it, the school nurse, Miss Blakeway, let out a scream – as, indeed, would anyone who had just met a boy whose entire face was a vivid, fluorescent yellow.

A fourth odd event concerned the trophy cabinet outside the headmaster's office. In it was a large bronze-coloured cup awarded annually to the pupil who won the school's popular end-of term general knowledge quiz. The name 'Gabrielle Grayling' had been engraved on the cup five times in a row, but the latest name to be added was not Gabby's but that of Abigail Pipit, a girl who Gabby was convinced had cheated on the quiz by photocopying the answer sheet and memorising it a week in advance. The bronze cup lay now on the floor in front of the cabinet. It appeared to have been stamped on and smashed almost beyond recognition. Oddly, the cabinet itself was still intact and locked. Odder still, and which would not be discovered yet for some while, the names engraved on the cup had mysteriously transformed into mirror writing.

CHAPTER NINE
INJURY TIME

The side of Barney's boot connected perfectly with the football. It made a *tump* sound. Barney loved that sound. It usually meant the ball was going to go exactly where he wanted it. In this case, he wanted the ball to sail majestically over the head of Adam Crabtree and just to the right of where Thomas Gilchrist, the goalkeeper, would dive, arms furiously outstretched, on to the cold dry mud of the goalmouth. And this is exactly what happened.

Thomas rose slowly to his feet and retrieved the ball from the net, muttering grimly in a Glaswegian accent.

'Top scoring, dude!' Barney's team captain, Nick Goodwin, yelled and clapped Barney on the back.

Barney winced.Nick was one of those kids who referred to everyone as *dude*, including his mother, all teachers, and even, when he was putting them on before a game, his football boots. But Barney hated it.

'Cheers,' said Barney and jogged back to his side's half of the pitch. He was not one for extravagant celebrations after scoring a goal. He didn't run around the pitch with his shirt over his head or slide spectacularly along the grass on his knees, arms raised. He preferred merely to nod with quiet satisfaction and maybe indulge in a dignified handshake or two with his teammates. Anything more looked like showing off – and that wasn't his style.

It was a bright, cold, early evening, perfect for football. Blue Hills High had sold its playing fields years ago so the school team always practised in the nearby park. They usually attracted a decent crowd while they were practising but the park was peculiarly empty this evening, with only the players' coats and schoolbags dotting the perimeter of the pitch.

'OK, dudes!' Nick called to his team. 'That makes two-all! One more goal, dudes! That's all we need! One more little goal! Let's do this, dudes!'

'Yeah, *dudes*,' called a mocking voice. Someone laughed. Nick ignored them.

The opposing team (who were, in fact, the other half of Blue Hills High's squad as this was a practice game) took their positions for kick-off. Their captain, a squat, cocky kid called Dan Perch, placed the ball on the centre spot. He intended to give it a swift kick almost immediately, passing to midfielder Rob Yellowwood, but when Dan drew back his leg he was astonished to find the ball had gone. Assuming some freakish gust of wind, he searched around for it, without success.

'Anyone seen the ... er ... *ball*?' he called out, feeling a bit of an idiot.

'Look!' cried someone.

'There!' shouted another.

'Blimey!' yelled someone else.

'Above your head!' bellowed a fourth.

Dan looked upwards and was dumbstruck to find the ball floating quite contentedly in the air about twenty centimetres above his head. Furious, he grabbed it with both hands, as if the ball were somehow misbehaving on purpose and showing him up in front of his friends. But it refused to budge, however hard he yanked it, remaining steadfastly in position in the air. In fact, he was able to lift himself clean off the ground by hanging on to it. Silently he mouthed the words 'What the flipping heck ...?' before letting go and dropping down on to the grass.

'Well,' said Barney, 'that's weird.'

Dan looked around at the other boys, finally regaining the power of speech. 'It's stuck. What do we do?'

'Stuck?' growled Thomas. 'It cannae be stuck in the air! That makes no sense!'

'Well, you come and move it then if you're so clever, Professor Stephen McHawking!' suggested Dan. 'I would love to see you have a go, I really would.'

Thomas strolled up to the floating ball. Barney had never seen him worried or intimidated by anyone or anything for as long as he'd known him and he didn't expect the big Scots lad to start freaking out now just because some pesky football was refusing to behave in the usual manner.

'Right, you,' said Thomas, staring hard at the football. 'Stop messing about and let us get on with our game!'

He leaped into the air in a great two-footed jump and planted his forehead against the ball with the force of a jackhammer. There was a loud *tump* noise not dissimilar to the one Barney was so fond of and Thomas's head rebounded backwards at enormous speed, toppling him over on to the ground in a dizzy heap.

The football remained hovering in the air, completely unmoved, and, as far as is possible for a football, looking a little aloof.

Some boys ran to see if Thomas was hurt. He shooed them away noisily and stared at the football with wide, terrified eyes, as if it were some hideous demon. 'That's no ball o' this Earth,' he hissed.

Nick now approached the ball, feeling, as captain of the school team and as there was no referee present, that he should take charge of the situation. 'Now look here, ball, dude,' he began in reasonable tones, assuming as Thomas had done that the ball had a mind of its own as well as the ability to defy gravity, 'we mean you no harm. I know we've kicked you about a bit – but we thought you didn't mind. We assumed, what with you being a football, you'd be OK with us treating you like–'

He didn't get to finish the sentence, at least not audibly to the others, because at that moment the ball suddenly lowered itself through the air and made contact with the top of Nick's head. There was another *tump* sound, softer this time, as the ball distorted, flattening as if squashed by a great weight, and then a *flomp* as it swallowed Nick's head completely.

The other boys now began seriously to freak out. Some ran away screaming; some ran up to Nick and tried to help him remove the football encasing his head. Nick himself wasn't helping matters, running in random directions, shouting muffled instructions to the other boys, gesticulating wildly and clawing, panic-stricken, at the football he was now wearing like a space helmet.

Barney watched as the football-headed boy ran blindly into a goalpost and bounced off it like a striker's poorly aimed shot. 'Bad luck,' he thought wryly. Then the seriousness of the situation hit home. Nick was almost certainly suffocating inside the football. Barney dashed to his schoolbag and fumbled in it for his pencil case. He drew out his compass, a blunt stubby pencil still clasped in its arm, and ran to Nick, who was lying on the ground just behind the goal, his skin a sickly bluish white and his legs kicking convulsively. Barney thrust the point of the compass into the top of the football and ripped, hoping the point would not spike the top of Nick's head. There was a loud *pop*! and the football burst, dropping on to the grass in a scraggy mess of torn plastic. Nick gasped for air, wheezing loudly. The colour slowly returned to his face.

'Thanks, dude,' he croaked at Barney.

'No worries, mate,' said Barney and helped him sit up. From the corner of his eye he noticed a bright flicker of light. Lightning? He waited for the thunder but none came. More explosions of brilliant light followed, like rapid bursts of a camera's flashbulb. Barney turned his head away and shielded his eyes with his arm. He could hear boys shouting in panic and confusion. What was going on now? He lowered his arm and blinked at the pitch. Rob Yellowwood had his arm around another boy, who was doing his best to hold back tears. The boy's lip was quivering uncontrollably.

'What's wrong?' called Barney, rising to his feet.

At the far end of the pitch there was another flash of white light and a startled yelp of surprise from one of the players.

'Stay back!' yelled Rob. 'Don't come on the pitch!'

Barney kept outside of the pitch's perimeter line. 'Why? What's up?'

'It's the lines on the pitch,' said Rob. 'We can't go outside the lines. Don't you come on and get stuck too.'

'What do you mean, you can't go outside the lines?'

'Watch,' said Rob. He strode towards Barney. As his foot crossed the white painted line marking the edge of the pitch, there was a flash of white light and Rob vanished. Barney gasped. A figure at the opposite end of the pitch waved at him. It was Rob. He jogged back up towards Barney.

'What just happened? You vanished!'

'Vanished as I crossed the line – appeared again back there. It's mad!' said Rob. 'Every time someone tries to leave the pitch, they end up vanishing and then reappearing on the opposite side!'

'Whoa,' said Barney. 'That's pretty messed up.'

'You're telling me,' said Rob. 'What the heck are we gonna do? I'm supposed to be going for a meal with my mum and dad and sister later. I don't want to be stuck on a football pitch for the rest of my life!'

Nick struggled to his feet. 'Stay there, dudes,' he wheezed. 'I'll go and get help,' adding, 'my dad's an engineer,' as if that explained everything. He sprinted towards the park gate.

'Stay here?' repeated Rob. 'Is he having a laugh? Like we have any choice.'

'Psssst! Barney!' hissed a voice.

Barney spun around. There was no one there. 'Hello?' he called uncertainly.

'Psssst! Over here.' It was Gabby's voice. And it was coming from a clump of trees not far from the pitch.

Barney approached it, a little warily. 'Gab? Is that you?'

'I'm here!' said Gabby's voice.

'Where?'

'In this tree.'

Shading his eyes against the low evening sun, Barney looked up into branches of the trees. There was no sign of Gabby.

'I can't see you . . .'

'Don't look up. Look at the trunk of the tree directly in front of you.'

Barney looked. Then he said a single word. A very bad word.

A moment passed.

'Ha!' said Gabby. 'That's pretty much the reaction I had earlier. Maybe the fourth dimension just has that effect on people.'

Barney nodded dumbly. The reason why he was so dumbstruck was that Gabby's face seemed to be protruding from the trunk of the tree in front of him. It wasn't that the tree was hollow and she was sticking her face out of a hole in the trunk. Her face seemed actually to be *growing* from the wood.

He ran his fingers over the rough bark of the

trunk and stopped when he reached Gabby's face. It was a normal, warm, fleshy human face and it was as embedded in the tree trunk as a firmly as chocolate chip in a cookie.

'Stop that!' smirked Gabby. 'It tickles.'

'Why is your face in a tree?' said Barney, mentally adding this question to his list of weird sentences no one in the history of the world had ever uttered before the creation of Geek Inc. 'Where's the rest of you?'

'In the fourth dimension!' said Gabby.

'In the *what*?'

'The rest of me is in another universe! I can enter ours at any point I like – even inside a solid object! Amazing, isn't it?'

'I'm starting to think someone might have slipped something a bit stronger into my pre-match energy drink,' said Barney, rubbing his eyes. 'It's been a very unusual day. What do you mean, the fourth dimension? I can't believe I'm talking to a tree.'

'I followed Chas earlier to find out what's going on with him, and it turns out he's from another dimension – the fourth dimension to be exact. That's why he can do all those impossible things. He's something called a hyperbeing – and actually the coolest boy I ever met, as it turns out.'

'Hang on,' said Barney firmly. 'Do you mean all the ...' he struggled to find the word '... *insanity* I've just witnessed on the football pitch – that was Chas?'

'No, silly,' said Gabby. 'That was me.'

'What?' said Barney. 'You put the football on Nick's head?'

The face in the tree giggled. 'Yes! Wasn't it hilarious? I've always thought he was a bit annoying – "dude" this and "dude" that.'

'And you did something to the pitch so no one can leave it?'

'I curved the surface of the pitch in the fourth dimension!' said Gabby proudly. 'It's a mini loop in the space-time continuum. Chas has shown me all sorts of cool things you can do from the fourth dimension, even just the small bit that we can get to.' She squinted at Barney. 'When I look at you from here in the other universe I can see thousands and thousands of Barneys, all lined up like paper dolls, each one a different layer of your body. I can see your skin, your nervous system, your blood, your organs, your bones. And I could reach out and touch them if I wanted.'

'Please don't.'

'Instead,' said Gabby, 'I'll do this!' A hand appeared in mid-air and clutched the top of Barney's right sock. It gave the sock a swift tug and removed it from his foot, pulling it through the solid material of his football boot as easily as a ghost walking through a wall. 'Ha ha!' The disembodied hand passed the sock to Barney and vanished.

Barney stared at the sock. His face started to colour.

'Good trick, eh?' said the face in the tree.

'Have you lost your mind, Gabby?' he all but screamed at her. 'You could have really hurt Nick. He nearly suffocated.' He pointed at the football pitch. 'Look at those boys. They're really scared! This is like some horrible nightmare! Why are you doing this?'

Gabby looked shocked. 'I never meant actually to *hurt* anyone,' she protested. 'It was only supposed to be a bit of mucking about.' The disembodied hand appeared again and waved at the football pitch. The air surrounding it seemed to shimmer like a summer heat haze. 'There. I've unbent the pitch. They're free to go.'

Barney paced about, shaking his head, toying with the sock in his hands. 'This isn't like you, Gab. And I don't just mean being inside a tree. What are you doing? The Gabby Grayling I know wouldn't harm someone else just for a cheap laugh. I don't understand it.'

Gabby sighed. 'No surprise there, then.'

'What do you mean?'

'Well, you're a nice lad and everything, Barney mate, but everything always comes as such a *surprise* to you.'

'Hey!' said Barney.

'The power of the fourth dimension that Chas has shown me is awesome, literally awesome. I feel like I could reach out and hold the entire Earth in the palm of my hand. And I understand it! The maths and physics behind all this is real – and I understand it! But you could never do that. I like you, but you're really the football-and-computer-games type rather than the intellectual adventurer, aren't you? What I'm doing here is way beyond your level. Maybe you don't really belong in Geek Inc. if your mind is that small and closed? I'm just saying.'

'Stop it!' said Barney. There were tears in his eyes. 'I like being in Geek Inc. with you. I like finding things out with you. I learn things from just hanging out with you.'

Gabby sniffed. 'Well, you certainly do have a lot to learn.'

'This is Chas, isn't it? He's messed with your mind somehow.'

'Don't say nasty things about Chas,' said Gabby sternly. 'He's so incredible. I'm going to help him get home. We've got a plan and the energy we need is right on the doorstep. Did you know he's asked me to visit him in his own universe, Barney? To see things no human being could ever conceive of? And I'm going. Oh yes. I might even stay. Doesn't look like I could cope with Blue Hills after what I've seen and done today. I need somewhere bigger.'

'You're losing it, Gabby,' said Barney softly. 'Listen to yourself. You're losing your mind.'

'Wrong,' said Gabby. 'I'm gaining one. A four-dimensional one. Oh – and by the way ...'

'Yes?'

'Sherlock Holmes is a fictional character, you moron! *He. Does. Not. Exist.*'

The face in the tree giggled and then vanished.

CHAPTER TEN
THE AGED HELP

Barney knocked hard on the door. After a short while there came from within the familiar creaking sound of Gill's walking frame. The door swung open.

'I need your help. It's important. Really, really important. Really, really, really important.'

Gill Abbott took a long drag on her cigarette and blew a stream of smoke into the evening air. 'I suppose you'd better come in then.'

She led him to the kitchen. Dave was sitting at

the table, peeling another apple. Gill filled the kettle. This gave Barney a mild sensation of déjà vu. He sat down opposite Dave.

'Thomas! Or is it Rufus? Bernard?'

'Barney.'

'Barney! Of course! Hello, son. How's things?'

'Not good, Dave. Not good at all.'

'Oh, dear!'

Gill looked at him with a concerned expression. 'What's wrong?'

Barney took a deep breath. 'I need help. Quite badly. And I think you're the only people who will understand.'

'How's that, Barney?' asked Dave. 'If there's anything we can do to help, of course we will.'

Barney looked at Gill. 'I've got a problem. A very odd problem. In fact, you could call it a *highly unusual* problem.'

Gill stared back. Her face was impossible to read.

'Highly unusual, eh?' said Dave. 'That used to be right up our street once. A long time ago.'

'What is it?' asked Gill. 'Can't be all that unusual, I'm sure.' She was trying to keep her voice light but Barney could detect a tremor of worry in it.

Barney stared at his hands. 'Please don't get upset at what I'm going to say. I'm not out to cause you any pain or rake up any bad memories. But it involves something seriously weird – a creature from another universe.'

He heard Gill's walking frame rattle violently. He looked up, expecting to find her looking angry or tearful again, but instead she was propelling herself towards the table as fast as she could. She sat down beside him and took his hand.

'Tell us about it.'

'My friend Gabby, the one I'm in Geek Inc. with, has met this boy. She says he's from the fourth dimension and somehow he's trapped in our world.

He can do incredible things and now she can too. But she was being really horrible to me and saying things that I know she wouldn't normally. I think the power she has is driving her crazy. I don't know what to do. You were the only people I could think of who would understand.' He turned to Dave. 'I found some of the documents from your Society of Highly Unusual Things in the stuff I was sorting through. I know you used to investigate stuff like this. And that you gave it up after your daughter vanished.'

'Good lord,' said Dave, staring into the distance. 'I haven't thought of Fleur, *really* thought of her in –' he paused, the half-peeled apple in his hands, '– twenty years or more. That's quite ridiculous, isn't it?'

'I think of her every day,' said Gill quietly. 'Every morning when I wake up. Sometimes I think you're lucky to be losing your memory.'

'This four-dimensional stuff,' said Barney gently, 'do you know anything about it?'

Gill nodded. 'All too well! This is how we lost Fleur. Opening doors to different universes. Doors open and people vanish through them. Forever. Stay well away, Barney. Have nothing to do with it.'

'But Gabby's my friend!' protested Barney. 'I can't sit back and watch this happen to her! She says she's going back with Chas once she helps him escape. What if she vanishes forever too?'

'A 4-D creature trapped in our world, eh?' said Dave, putting his apple down. 'How fascinating! Just the kind of thing we would have loved back in the day. How's your friend planning to help it escape?'

'I don't know. She said something about having the energy close by.'

Dave snapped his fingers. 'That's right. It takes a tremendous amount of energy to open a gateway to another universe. There's only one place in Britain that could provide it.'

'And where's that?' asked Barney.

'The new experimental fusion reactor at Sanderling Ridge. It's only about twenty miles from Blue Hills. Pound to a penny that's where your friend is headed.'

'I need to get there,' said Barney. 'I need to speak to her. Make her see sense.'

'Take me with you,' said Dave. 'I can help.'

'Don't talk rubbish!' spat Gill sourly. '"Take me with you" indeed! You can't even remember where the front door is, Dave! What use are you?'

'We were investigating four-dimensional gateways when Fleur disappeared,' said Dave. 'We know about them. We can help the lad.'

Gill stubbed out her cigarette. 'Huh. I'd be astonished if you remember anything at all about them, Brain of Britain.'

Dave picked up his apple and threw it at the washing-up rack next to the sink with the force of a cricket fielder. A neat line of flowery plates and mugs drying on the rack exploded into thick white-edged shards that clattered into the sink and on to the floor.

'Dave! What's got into you? Look at the plates!' Gill yelled.

'Stop treating me like I'm some sort of dribbling fool!' Dave exploded. 'The boy needs help, and you and I can give it to him. I am in the unusual position for the first time in thirty-odd years of being *useful* to someone – and you're not going to stop me!'

'But Dave, you can't–'

'No, Gill. We gave up the Society of Highly Unusual Things because we were afraid of causing harm. But here's an opportunity to use that knowledge to do some good!'

'Dave, you're shouting at me ...'

'I FEEL like shouting!' bellowed Dave. 'For the first time in ages I feel like shouting and running about and using my brain! Anything except mouldering away in this kitchen eating ruddy apples! Are we going to help the boy or what?'

Gill stared at her husband for a long time. 'Yes,' she said finally, in a quiet voice. 'Yes, you're right, darling. We've got to help Barney. Of course we have.'

'Thank you,' said Barney, feeling relieved to have someone on his side. 'So. What do we do? You mentioned this fusion plant, Dave?'

Dave nodded. 'Produces huge quantities of energy. It's what this 4-D beast will be after. Could be very dangerous if that energy is released suddenly.'

'How dangerous?'

'You ever hear of a couple of places called Hiroshima and Nagasaki?'

Barney nodded grimly. 'Pretty dangerous, then. Great. Is there anything we can do?'

'There is, as it happens,' said Gill. 'A few weeks before Fleur vanished, back in nineteen seventy-six, Dave and I had been researching reports of inter-dimensional rifts throughout history. It seems that in various places and various times, pathways have opened up between our world and different universes. There's a famous story from seventeen seventy-four about the chemist Joseph Priestley seeing a coach and horses vanish in a flash of light along Oxford Street in London. And lots of people have reported seeing things that can't really be there, which might be the same phenomenon. From what we could tell, a lot of these pathways were opened up by special objects – boxes, bits of furniture, books sometimes, but more often than not they were in lockets that people wore around the neck.'

'We found information on several of these lockets,' said Dave, hauling himself from his chair and picking up the chunks of broken pottery. Barney went to help him. 'They were called angel lockets because people thought they opened up doors to heaven. Needless to say, they were extremely rare. But the idea sort of took hold of us. We became obsessed with finding one.'

'We'd buy any old lockets from junk shops,' said Gill. 'Bought dozens of them. But of course they were just old lockets. Nothing more. The last one I found I couldn't open. It drove me mad because I could tell there was some simple knack to the clasp that held the two halves together. I fiddled with that damn locket for two solid days. Then when I did open it—'

'It was at the park, wasn't it?' Barney cut in. 'When the mayor was unveiling that statue?'

Gill nodded. 'The locket opened. There was a white light. And Fleur vanished.'

'And that was when the statue got reversed, wasn't it?'

'Some force from the fourth dimension nudged the statue,' said Dave, 'rotating it about a 4-D axis, turning it into its own mirror image.'

'But how could it do that?' asked Barney.

Dave held up a plate, one of the few on the draining board that was still in one piece. Painted on it was a picture of Big Ben and the Houses of Parliament. 'See this plate? See the picture on it?'

'Yup.'

Dave turned the plate over in his hands. 'Well, I can rotate the plate two ways – forwards and backwards, and from side to side. When it's upside down it looks different, doesn't it? But it's still the same plate.'

'Obviously.'

'Obviously. But there's another way I could rotate the plate if I were able to. Through the fourth dimension. It's not a direction we humans have access to normally, but if I did, I would be able to rotate the plate so that when we looked at it we saw it as a mirror image of itself. Do you see?'

'And that's what happened to the statue?'

'That's right.'

'Shall I stick the plate away in the cupboard now? I don't think it actually belongs in the cutlery drawer where you're putting it.'

Dave chuckled. 'Thank you, Barney.'

'If we gave the locket to the four-dimensional creature,' reasoned Gill, 'it could use it to go home without having to absorb the energy of the fusion reactor. And if we were very careful, no one need get hurt at all.' She put a hand to her throat and lifted a thin silver chain from around her neck. Dangling from it was a small silvery shape. She handed it to Barney.

'You've still got the locket?' Barney stared at it in awe. He felt like he was holding a very small but immensely powerful bomb.

'Couldn't get rid of it, risk someone else vanishing into it. Far too dangerous. And it reminds me of Fleur. Maybe it can do some good today for once.'

'We should get going,' said Dave. 'We can't afford to hang about. Too much is at stake.'

'How are we going to get there?' asked Barney. 'It's twenty miles away.'

'We've got our bus passes,' said Gill. 'Have you got enough money for the fare, Barney?'

'What?' He looked at her, momentarily dumbfounded. 'Uh, yeah. I guess. But isn't there any quicker way of–'

Gill and Dave looked at one another and suddenly burst out laughing. Slowly and painfully, Gill rose to her feet. She hobbled with her walking frame over to a kitchen cupboard and fished out a key from a bowl. She held it up for Barney to see.

'This is the key to a nineteen seventy-three Ford Cortina XLE. She hasn't been out of our garage for nearly fifteen years, but every weekend we give her a polish and start her up just to hear the engine.'

'Her name's Daisy,' explained Dave.

'And you haven't driven her for fifteen years?'

'We've never had anywhere to go,' said Dave.

'Until now,' said Gill. 'Come on.'

'Are you sure you're both up to it?' asked

Barney, eyeing them uncertainly. 'I mean, I don't mean to be rude or anything but neither of you are as young as you once were ...'

Gill kicked over her walking frame violently. It clattered to the kitchen floor. 'Time's a-wasting,' she said. 'Let's hit the road. Geek Inc. and the Society of Highly Unusual Things have a problem to solve.'

CHAPTER ELEVEN
SANDERLING RIDGE

It was a clear, chilly evening and the two massive cooling towers stood silent and brooding like twin giants surveying the vast stretch of barren countryside that formed their kingdom. They rose amidst a complex of buildings – boxy control rooms, pipe-sprouting reprocessing facilities, vast cathedral-sized turbine halls and an enormous hexagonal-patterned reactor dome resembling a gigantic golf ball half buried in the earth.

High in a plush office in one of the buildings,

working late for the fourth night in a row, Julia Goosefoot, the general manager of Sanderling Ridge (formerly Cherrycroft Mount, formerly Lark Meadows, formerly Dandelion Grove) sat at a desk and stared lovingly at a framed photograph of a handsome man and two extremely cute kids. The man wasn't her husband and the kids weren't hers – in fact it was a photograph she had cut out of an advert for biscuits in the magazine that came with her Sunday paper. But she loved the photograph anyway because it made visitors to her office think she was normal. And when people thought she was normal that gave her an advantage over them – because in reality there was very little that was normal about Julia Goosefoot. She was, to pick just three things at random, abnormally cruel, abnormally single-minded and abnormally ambitious.

At the age of four, Julia had attached roller skates to her sleeping grandmother's garden chair and sent the old woman trundling down a hill towards a busy road, just so she could steal her grandmother's last slice of toast. Fortunately, a neighbour had managed to intercept the runaway chair seconds before it entered traffic and returned it safely to the Goosefoot family's garden before the old woman had even woken up.

When she was seven, she climbed into an enclosure at Chester Zoo and threw a baby porcupine at a teacher who had told her off for speaking with her mouth full.

When she was twelve, she filled a friend's aquarium with coffee to make the fish swim faster – they had, apparently, been swimming far too slowly for her liking. Her parents had to buy replacements for all the fish she poisoned.

When she was twenty, she was banned from her local library for hollowing out a set of encyclopaedias and filling them with worms as a practical joke. The first person to open one of these doctored encyclopaedias – a retired hat salesman from Stockport – had fainted clean away when he had tried to look up the capital of Peru and found a mass of wriggling worms inside the book.

A year later, serving a six-month stretch in prison for spraying milkshake at the guards outside Buckingham Palace, she came to the attention of the owners of a new nuclear power plant called Dandelion Grove near the small north-west town of Blue Hills. There had recently been a series of radiation leaks at the plant which had resulted in an awful lot of bad publicity, the changing of the plant's name several times to distract the public, and the sacking of the plant's general manager. The owners were now looking for someone to take over. The only qualification necessary was that the new manager be as nasty and horrible a human being as they could possibly find – in order to scare the workforce into working harder and more safely, and to scare the press into not asking too many probing questions about the plant. When they read in the newspaper about Julia Goosefoot and her history of appalling wrongdoing, they offered her the job immediately on her leaving prison, and were delighted to find that she was very good at it indeed.

Julia adjusted the photograph on her desk so that she could see the bland smiling faces a little better. Had these people actually been her family, she thought, they would be proud of her.

About a mile from the plant, on a bleak stretch of moorland, Chas and Gabby re-entered our universe. Gabby reeled, open-mouthed, afraid she was about to lose her balance. Seeing the layers of soft bracken and spongy moss beneath her feet, she let herself fall to the ground, giggling. She stared up at the darkening sky and the few evening stars that were emerging tentatively from it.

'The word "wow",' she said, 'is so small, so useless, so totally incapable of expressing how absolutely *wooooooooooowwww* I feel right now. I may need some time to think of another word for the job.' She giggled again.

'What you've experienced so far,' said Chas, 'is tiny. An infinitesimally small area of hyperspace. Merely the bit of my universe that touches yours. Once I'm able to move freely in the fourth dimension again, then we can *really* go places.'

'Just looking at ordinary stuff from your world – a leaf, a stone, the sunset … So much beauty in the must mundane things! I don't think my head's big enough to fit all this wonderfulness in,' Gabby said.

Chas smirked. 'Your head's pretty big already, I reckon.'

'Hey!' She sat up and thumped him playfully. As she did she caught sight of the fusion plant in the distance, its bold geometric shapes resembling an oversized version of a toddler's building blocks. 'We're here! What do we do?'

'We wait a moment.'

'What for?'

'There! Watch!'

'Where?'

Chas shrugged. 'Everywhere, pretty much.'

'Huh?'

Gabby got to her feet and looked around – and then she saw. All over the moor, in every direction, in hundreds and hundreds of separate locations, boys were appearing – hands, noses, knees forming in mid-air, then thickening into arms, torsos, heads and legs. Chases – hundreds of copies of Chas wearing school uniforms of all colours – were creating themselves out of nothing.

Once fully formed, they turned as one and marched towards Chas and Gabby, a silent army. Gabby squeaked in alarm.

'Don't worry,' said Chas. 'It's only me.'

'I know,' said Gabby. 'But there's an awful lot of you.'

'To break through completely into the fourth

dimension I'll need to concentrate all the energy of the reactor into a single space.'

'What does that mean?

In reply, Chas merely smiled enigmatically and stood with his arms outstretched. A white ghostlike glow appeared around him.

The first of the duplicates arrived. It winked at Gabby and touched Chas's outstretched hand. The duplicate vanished and the white light around Chas pulsed and grew stronger. Soon, more duplicates drew near, touching Chas's hands in turn and disappearing, causing Chas's aura to grow and pulsate further. Gabby sensed the duplicates were somehow merging with him. In the space of a minute, all the duplicates had made contact with Chas and evaporated. The glow around him was now a strong silvery gleam that lit up the desolate landscape around them.

Five hundred kilometres above, a satellite's camera whirred silently.

Chas looked at Gabby and grinned. His bright silvery aura gave him the look of some restless Greek god come down to Earth to cause mischief. 'We need to get inside the reactor now. It's time.'

'How do we do that? Another shortcut through the fourth dimension?'

Chas nodded. 'This will be the last one for a little while. In this somewhat energetic state I'm in at the moment –' he flapped his arms a couple of times, leaving feathery streams of white energy billowing in their wake, '– it's too risky to keep hopping from one universe to another. With all the power of the duplicates concentrated within me, my molecules are all a bit unstable.'

Gabby's eyes widened. 'You're not in any danger though, are you?'

'No. I'll be fine.' He held out a hand to her. His long fingers left little vapour trails like comets.

Gabby took it.

*

'There! That light! Did you see that? Head for it!'
Barney pointed a decisive finger into the distance
as the old Cortina rattled along the narrow road.

Beside him at the wheel, Gill nodded. 'Same
kind of light we saw when Fleur disappeared. Well,
a weaker version, anyway.' She slammed her foot
on the accelerator and Daisy sped forwards
through the darkness.

'Harland radiation,' said Barney.

'What's that?' came Dave's voice from the back
of the car. Minutes after setting off he had been
struck down with a headache and decided to
have a lie down. The back seat was not the most
comfortable of beds and he was rattling about like
a dried pea in a maraca.

'I fished a bunch of documents out of the
recycling bin,' said Barney, holding up a sheaf of
papers. 'One of them's about the angel lockets.
Thought it might be useful. This one says the
bright flashes of light that accompany the

opening of doorways to higher dimensions are caused by Harland radiation.'

'Ah, yes,' said Dave. 'The hole between dimensions sends out ripples of gravity that our eyes interpret as white light.'

'That's exactly what it says here!' said Barney. 'I think your memory's improving, Dave!'

'Thanks, Rufus!'

'It's Barney.'

'Damn.'

There was another burst of light, a fierce yellow glare that hurt their eyes. It was very near. There came a second and then a third. These weren't sudden flashes, though, like the light they had seen earlier. These were powerful searchlightlike beams that cut like sabres through the darkness towards them. They were more like the headlights of cars, Barney realised. But what would a bunch of cars be doing here in the middle of the moor?

'Halt! Stop the vehicle or I fire!' called a voice through a loudhailer.

Gill looked at Barney uncertainly.

'Probably best not to disobey someone who ends a request with "or I fire",' said Barney. 'Stop the car.'

Gill brought Daisy to a halt and switched off the ignition. They could hear the sound of running feet and frantically revving engines outside. Blazing beams of torchlight crisscrossed the sky.

'Step out of the vehicle!' commanded the loudhailer.

Barney shot Dave a quick glance. Dave nodded and kept as low as possible on the back seat. Gill opened the door and began to climb out. 'Hold your horses,' she called to the unseen owner of the loudhailer. 'I'm not as young as I once was, so it may take a moment or two ...'

Barney quickly got out of the car and scooted around to help Gill. Torchlight blasted their eyes.

'Freeze!' called the loudhailer voice.

'On a moor at this time of night in just a cardigan – I probably will,' said Gill, squinting into the torch beams.

'The prisoners will desist in making sarcastic comments!' commanded the voice.

'Why are we prisoners?' asked Barney. 'There's nothing illegal about going for a night-time drive near an experimental nuclear reactor, is there?' He paused. 'Mind you, put like that it does sound a bit suspicious.'

'Good evening,' said Gill, changing tack and giving a charming smile. 'I'm afraid we're in rather a hurry. And as you can see, we're not terrorists, so ...'

'How do I know you're not terrorists?' asked the voice.

'We're just an old lady and a kid,' said Gill. 'A wild guess tells me we don't fit the usual profile of people who'd want to blow up a reactor.'

'Then it's the perfect cover, isn't it?' said the voice.

'What?' said Gill.

'If you wanted to blow up this reactor, who better to send than some harmless old granny and a dozy-looking kid? Terrorists aren't stupid, you know.'

'Who are you calling dozy-looking?' asked Barney. 'And you might as well know we're actually here to stop the reactor being blown up.'

'Barney's right,' said Gill. 'There are immense and dangerous forces at work on the moor tonight and if we can't–'

'Hang on,' interrupted the voice. 'Did you say Barney? As in Barney Watkins? From Blue Hills?'

'Erm, yes,' said Barney. 'How do you know who I am? Who–'

The dazzling torchlight snapped off and a tall dark figure marched out of the darkness towards Gill and Barney. When the after-images had stopped jigging across Barney's retinas, the figure suddenly resolved itself into a shape he recognised.

'Orville?' said Barney. 'Is that you?'

'You know this person?' asked Gill.

'He works for the government,' said Barney. 'He helped sort out some weird stuff in Blue Hills last year. Orville's a friend of Gabby's dad.'

'*Sir* Orville now, actually,' replied the figure. 'I might have known you were mixed up in this somehow. And where's your partner-in-mischief? I daresay Miss Gabrielle Grayling has a hand in proceedings too?'

Barney nodded. 'Yup. We reckon she's in the power plant. With a very dangerous creature from another universe. If we don't get to her soon we're afraid there may be consequences – the sort that end with a "boom" noise.'

'You know of the hyperbeings?' Orville McIntyre's face creased into a grim, heavy-shadowed mask in the dim light.

'Sure do,' said Barney. 'I've sat behind one in my maths class for the past four weeks.'

'What? There's been one in your school? The whole world is in danger! You realise these things are as powerful as gods?'

Barney nodded. 'Yeah, and he's a bit of a show-off, too, if you ask me. We need to go and speak to him and Gabby. Right now.'

'Our satellite picked up traces of something called Harland radiation at this location,' said McIntyre. 'It's something that accompanies the opening of doors to other dimensions. Now we know why. This really is most worrying.' He clicked his fingers and two armed military policemen strode forward through the darkness. He nodded to Gill and Barney. 'These two people will be accompanying us into the plant, and by "people" I actually mean "prisoners". By "accompanying us into the plant" I actually mean "will stay close to us at all times or risk ending the evening with considerably more bullet holes in them than when they started out". Everyone understand?'

CHAPTER TWELVE
FOUR DREADFUL THINGS

Gabby materialised inside a large hexagonal room. She caught her breath and took in her surroundings while her senses readjusted to three-dimensional space. The room was walled with pale green metal panels and contained a single massive control console. There was something reassuringly sturdy and old-fashioned about its rows of switches, dials, flashing lights and computer monitors, she thought. It inspired confidence in the same way that a vintage car does. She guessed it was the reactor's main control centre. Though Chas had been sketchy on the actual details of his plan beyond saying he would 'concentrate the plant's energy into a single space', she began to feel more confident that he would succeed in escaping from Earth.

Then she saw the *things*.

Things was the only word Gabby could think to call the ... *things* ... she was now looking at. There were four of them. They were sort of person-sized and sort of person-shaped but considerably more blurry and nightmarish than the average person generally prefers to look. Shifting columns of grey-pink light, they twisted and writhed like jellyfish, faceless as processed meat.

'You may be wondering what those ... *things* ... are,' said a tinny voice.

Gabby tore her gaze away from the four dreadful *things* and saw an image of Chas on one of the computer monitors. He was wreathed in his silvery glow and appeared to be floating in a tank of bubbling water.

'Hi,' she said. 'And yes, I am wondering that. I'm also wondering why you seem to be doing an impression of a green bean in a saucepan.'

Chas chuckled. 'First things first. Let me explain. The four *things* you can see in the control room there are the four members of staff who were working here when we arrived.'

Gabby looked aghast. 'What? What have you done to them?'

'It's OK! They're not being harmed. You remember when you folded the football pitch through the fourth dimension and no one could leave it?'

'You've folded these people?'

'I've folded the space immediately around them. Whenever they try to move more than a few centimetres, they reappear back where they started. It's just my way of keeping them out of our hair while we go about our business. And a bit classier than clunking them on the head with a spanner and tying them up, eh?'

'I see,' said Gabby. She shivered. The explanation did nothing to make the four *things* any less unsettling to look at. 'And the reason you're scuba diving in an enormous kettle is ...?'

'I'm in the main reactor itself,' replied Chas. 'This water I'm in is superheated and super-pressurised. No being from your world could survive in here, of course, but to me it's just like dipping your toe in a lovely cool pond.'

'I'm glad you're having a relaxing time of it,' said Gabby. 'Tell me what I have to do.'

The image of Chas on the monitor grew larger until his face filled the entire screen. 'We're going to overload the reactor, Gabby. To do that we'll need to bypass all the safety features. Basically there's a whole load of buttons on the control console you need to press and then a few commands to type into one of the computer terminals. You understand?'

'Pushing buttons and using computers are the things I like doing anyway,' said Gabby. 'So the fact I can do those things *and* help free an amazing hyperbeing from a dimensional trap is a bit of a bonus. In many ways this is my ideal job.'

They both laughed.

Chas stared at Gabby through the monitor screen. His flick of blond hair twisted and swirled in the boiling water. 'You are the most incredible three-dimensional creature I've ever met, Gabby.'

She felt herself blush. 'You're the most incredible four-dimensional creature I've ever met. Not to say the only one.'

'I'm not kidding,' said Chas. 'Out of all the hundreds of schools I was in, only you thought to investigate me. You're a special and unique kind of girl.'

Gabby remembered with a twinge of guilt how

Barney had wanted to investigate Chas too. She pushed the thought from her mind. 'I'm not all that special, you know.'

'You're a rare kind of spirit. You know that. This world can't contain you, Gabby. Come with me. For a visit, at least.'

'I'd love to! The last place I went on holiday was Southport. I imagine the fourth dimension is even more exciting.'

'That's pretty tough competition,' laughed Chas. 'You'll just have to wait and see. Are you ready, then? Shall we do this momentous thing?'

'Absolutely!'

'Right. You see that row of red buttons across the middle of the main console?'

'Uh-huh.'

'Press them all in turn. Starting from the left. That will disable all the reactor's safety systems.'

Gabby found the buttons and did as Chas asked. After she pressed the fifth one, an ear-splitting siren filled the control room. She squealed in fright and looked at the computer monitor questioningly.

'Don't worry about that!' shouted Chas above the din. 'It's just the overload alarm. Keep pressing the buttons. It'll go off when you press the ... ah! –' the alarm ceased abruptly '– when you press the last button. Good! Now, look at the second computer screen on the left. Go to the keyboard and type the words "deactivate safety features". Got that?'

'Got it.' Gabby's fingers danced lightly over the computer keyboard. 'Now what?'

'You should see a little red icon on the screen now called "overload". Can you see it?'

'Yep.'

'All you have to do is copy that icon into the folders on the desktop called "reactors". They should be numbered one to five.'

'Okey-dokey.' She quickly copied the icon and began pasting it into the five folders. 'All done.'

'Great! All you have to do now is reboot the entire system.'

'Righto. Won't that alarm have attracted attention from the other workers here?'

'Not a problem,' said Chas. 'They'll be dead in a few seconds once this reactor blows. Now, you can do the system reboot from the start menu like any normal computer–'

'*What?*'

'Just click on the thing that says "start" in the bottom left-hand corner of the screen.'

'No, not that,' said Gabby. 'What was that about the reactor blowing up and killing people? Are you serious?'

'Yeah,' said Chas casually. 'It'll be quite a bang. Should take out everything within a – oooh – thirty-mile radius, I should think. Be pretty spectacular.'

'That's monstrous! I can't do that!'

'Why not?'

'Why not?' hooted Gabby. 'Are you completely mad? I'm not going to cause a massive explosion!'

Chas laughed. 'It's OK, Gabby. I'll protect you. Once I've absorbed the energy of the fusion reaction I can quickly slip you into the fourth dimension where the blast can't touch you. You'll be fine. I probably should have mentioned that earlier.'

'But what about everyone else within a thirty-mile radius? The people who work in this plant? The people in Blue Hills? My mum?'

Chas shrugged. 'Well they'll all be blasted to smithereens of course. Shall we continue?'

'You're totally out of your mind if you think I'm going to help you kill every single person within a thirty-mile radius!' Gabby stepped back from the console. 'Is there no other way at all to get you back home?'

'Honestly, what are you so concerned about?'

asked Chas impatiently. 'A few thousand measly three-dimensional creatures will be killed in the explosion. But so what? How many insects and other small creatures do you think were killed when they built this plant? How many animals are killed every day to feed human beings? Or what about this – how many microscopic creatures like bacteria is your own immune system killing *right now* as we speak, Gabby? Hmm? Think about it. Inside your blood stream right now, white blood cells are killing millions and millions of innocent bacteria, viruses and parasites. Tiny little creatures just trying to get on with their day like anyone else – and you're killing them. Do you feel sympathy for the common cold virus when your immune system destroys it? Of course not. So why should I feel sympathy for a few human beings?'

'Excuse me!' said Gabby indignantly. 'You're talking about my mum!'

'You won't need a mum where we're going!' said Chas. 'You won't need anything from this petty ant farm of a world. You'll be a god! It doesn't get much cooler than that, does it?'

'I'm not interested in being cool,' said Gabby. 'Never have been. Anyone who really knew me would know that.' With a pang, she suddenly thought of Barney again. 'I'm not going to help you.' She headed for the control room door.

'If you step through that door I'll die, Gabby. I'm stuck inside this tank now until the reactor overloads and gives me its power. But I can't survive in here indefinitely and if this bit of me in your universe dies, it will spread to my four-dimensional body and that'll be the end of me.'

Gabby raised her eyebrows. 'You should have thought of that earlier, shouldn't you, clever-clogs? Why should all those people die to save you?'

'Don't let me die!' All Chas's cockiness was

gone now. 'I can contain the explosion. It doesn't have to kill anyone. I promise. I can do it. Please.'

'Really? You promise?'

'Absolutely, Gabby! I promise. Please forgive me. I'm sorry I got a bit carried away just then. I didn't mean any of that nasty stuff. I'm just scared, that's all.'

She headed back to the computer console. 'OK, Chas. Let's do this.'

'Thank you! Whew! That was scary for a moment! Glad we're mates again!'

In the reactor tank, Chas smiled with relief and uncrossed his fingers.

Sometime earlier, Orville McIntyre, his guard of four military policemen, and his two prisoners, Gill and Barney, had swept through the security checks at the main entrance to Sanderling Ridge like a bolt of lightning in a hurry. Seeing McIntyre's laminated government security card, signed by the

Prime Minister himself, the plant's security guards transformed in an instant from surly bulldog-faced bruisers into simpering toads. One guard even offered them a homemade raspberry flan his wife had baked for his tea break. Eyeing the confection, McIntyre accepted it with a gracious smile and handed it to Barney.

'Carry this for me, would you? I should be extremely grateful – and people to whom I have reason to be grateful have a habit of living longer than those who don't.'

'Excuse me?'

'Just carry the flan, boy.'

Barney frowned. McIntyre had acted a little sniffy and superior last time they had met, but now there was something far more calculating and single-minded about him, something almost snakelike. He didn't like it one little bit.

They hurried through a maze of winding corridors until they came to a door marked *Fusion*

Reactor – Central Control Complex. Strictly No Admittance to Unauthorised Personnel. Pointing at the sign, McIntyre chuckled. 'Ooh, how scary. We're going to get in awful trouble if we go through here, lads. I hope you're all feeling extra brave.'

The four military policemen laughed. Gill looked at Barney and rolled her eyes. 'Stupid men,' she muttered, her thin shoulders heaving as she panted for breath. Her face was red and smeared with sweat. 'Everything's a joke to them.'

'Are you all right?' asked Barney.

Gill nodded. 'I think so. But if I ever get access to a time machine – which in Blue Hills is probably likelier than you might think – I'm going to meet myself aged eleven and convince myself not to take up smoking.' She put a hand to her mouth and coughed.

Barney spluttered. '*Eleven?*'

'Yes. I was a late developer.'

McIntyre tried the handle of the door. It was

locked. He stood aside and nodded to the chief of his military guard, Captain Grebe. The burly military policeman raised a brutish-looking sub-machine gun and aimed it at the door lock.

'I'd cover your ears if I were you, Barney,' advised McIntyre. 'In this enclosed space the gunshots will be pretty loud. Wouldn't want you to go deaf.' He turned to Gill. 'Probably a bit late in your case, isn't it?' He tittered childishly.

Gill folded her arms. 'Cheeky so-and-so. You think you're so clever, don't you?'

McIntyre nodded. 'Indeed I do, madam. Between you and me, I am something of a super-genius. So great is my brainpower, in fact, that I have very recently been promoted to a position that makes me the eighth most powerful person in the entire world.'

'Oh, really? Watch this.'

Gill hobbled towards the door. Barney and McIntyre exchanged a curious glance. McIntyre waved a hand and Captain Grebe lowered his gun. Gill turned the handle and pulled open the door in a single easy movement. She tapped a gnarled finger on a second notice halfway down the door that read *Please Pull to Open*.

'Does this make me the seventh most powerful person in the world?'

'A shrewd observation,' said McIntyre. 'Well done, dear lady. Where would we all be without the wisdom of our elders, eh?' He smiled curtly and walked through the open door. His smile evaporated a second later when he was hit on the back of the head with a very expensive handbag. He crumpled to the ground in a rotund heap of pinstripe.

Barney, Gill and the military policemen hurried through the door to find the owner of the expensive handbag – a tall thin blonde woman in a smart business suit – standing over McIntyre. She was brandishing a revolver.

'What in the name of heaven are you people doing here?' she demanded, waving the gun wildly. The hands of the four military police went straight to their weapons. 'The name's Julia Goosefoot and I run this place. Explain yourselves.'

'We're trying to stop this place being blown up,' said Barney. 'We need to get to the main control room right now.'

'The boy's right,' muttered McIntyre from the floor, clutching his bruised head.

'You seriously expect me to believe that?' said Julia. She pressed the end of the revolver against Barney's nose. He quivered. 'I think you're here to steal nuclear secrets. There's a lot of foreign powers would like to know what happens in Sanderling Ridge. Oh yes.'

Gill shoved the barrel of the gun away from Barney's nose. 'What do you think you're doing, pointing guns at a young boy? You ought to be ashamed.'

Julia now pressed the gun against Gill's forehead. Gill met her gaze steadily. 'And who are you exactly? James Bond's granny?'

'Put down your weapon, miss,' commanded Captain Grebe.

'You heard him,' said McIntyre, wheezing and puffing as he got to his feet. 'Lose the gun, dear lady.'

'Oh really?' said Julia. 'You'll shoot me, won't you? What if I *won't* put down my weapon?'

Captain Grebe and the other three military policemen went into a huddle. After a few seconds, Captain Grebe spoke. 'We realise we can't *make* you put down your weapon so we're just asking *nicely* if you wouldn't mind putting it down? Could you do that?'

'No. You've still got your guns. That's a little unfair. How about we all put our guns down at the same time?'

Captain Grebe looked at his three colleagues.

They nodded. 'Yes,' he said. 'That works for us. Shall we do it after "three"?'

'Fine,' said Julia. 'One ... two ...' She began to place her revolver delicately on the floor.

'Three!' said the military policemen and threw down their sub-machine guns.

With sudden speed, Julia scooped up her revolver and pointed it at the others. 'Ha!' she cried. 'Not so clever now, are we? OK, lads. I want to know exactly who you are and what you're doing here.' She waved the gun threateningly. 'Stay away from the weapons and start talking!'

'Good grief,' muttered McIntyre. 'We could be here all night.' He made a sudden dive for Julia's legs and rugby-tackled her to the ground. 'Help me get her gun!' he called to the others. Barney, Gill and the four military policemen rushed to McIntyre's aid. There began a great wriggling scramble of limbs on the ground with much pushing, shoving and shouting. Seven pairs of hands strained for the gun.

A shot rang out, devastatingly loud. Barney fell to the floor. The others continued their frenzied struggling.

'Barney!' cried Gill. She pulled the boy away from the scrum of bodies. Blood was streaming from a wound in the centre of his chest. His eyes were half closed.

'Huh ...?' he muttered.

'It's OK,' said Gill, trying to keep the sob from her voice. 'You'll be fine, son. Just take it easy.' She cradled his head, desperately trying to remember the first aid she had learned as a young woman. She needed something to staunch the flow of blood ... anything. Quickly, she removed her cardigan and pressed it gently to his chest. A tear splashed on to Barney's forehead.

'Umm, I'm OK, actually,' he said, trying to get up.

'No, don't move,' said Gill, easing him back to the floor. She pulled a mobile phone from the pocket of her cardigan and began fiddling with it inexpertly. 'You're so brave, aren't you? Poor, poor boy. We'll get you an ambulance ... as soon as I can remember how to turn this blasted phone on. Hush now.'

Barney wrested himself from Gill's grip and stood up. 'Get *off*. I'm fine. The gunshot missed me. This isn't blood. It's juice from that raspberry flan.'

Gill blinked. 'Oh.' A thought struck her. 'Are you saying I just ruined my best cashmere cardigan for nothing?'

The others were still struggling madly with Julia Goosefoot for possession of the gun. Barney and Gill watched with horrified bemusement. Gill tapped Barney on the shoulder. 'Now would be a good time to nip away.'

Barney nodded.

They scurried around a corner and along another corridor, arriving eventually at a staircase.

A sign on the wall told them it led to the main reactor control room on the fifth floor.

'Up here,' said Barney, bounding up the stairs two at a time.

'Yeah, *right*,' called Gill's voice behind him. There was a 'ping' noise and the sound of automatic doors opening. 'I don't know about you but I'm taking the lift.'

Gabby clicked the 'restart' icon. The various coloured windows and charts on the screen began to vanish one by one. 'It's done.'

'Faberoony,' came Chas's voice from the computer monitor. 'It'll take a few minutes for the reactor to reach its critical temperature. Then we're off to the races. And don't you worry. The explosion won't hurt you at all. You have my word.'

'I thought you said there wasn't going to be an explosion any more?' said Gabby, her stomach suddenly seeming to fill with jagged shards of ice. 'I thought you were going to contain it all?'

On the screen, Chas grinned guiltily. 'Yeah, I did say that, didn't I? You wouldn't have helped me otherwise. Sorry, Gabby. Looks like there's going to be a bit of a bang after all.'

'You lied to me!'

'Yes, but *very well*. You must admit that.'

'You're a monster!'

'Oh, don't get hysterical,' said Chas. 'You'll soon forget this cardboard cut-out world once you get to my universe. Your mind is going to be blown on a daily basis there, believe me.'

Gabby swept the computer keyboard off the console. It clattered to the floor. 'Do you think I care about your stupid universe? This is where I live. This is where everyone I care about lives! Stop this explosion, Chas. *Please!*'

Chas pretended to consider for a moment. 'Er ... no. I won't. I'm going home. And you're coming with me, like it or not. You'll be my cute three-dimensional pet. I've always wanted one. I'll be able to show you off to my friends. They'll find you fascinating. But then, lower forms of life always are, aren't they?'

Gabby turned her face away from the monitor to hide her tears.

The door flew open. She spun around on her chair. Through her misted, hair-straggled glasses she saw two figures enter the room. One of them appeared to be wearing a bright red shirt or waistcoat and for an absurd moment she thought the pair had come in fancy dress as Bobby Robin and Cluedroid from *The Robin and the Robot*.

'It's OK, Gab. We're here now.'

'Barney!'

Gabby raced up and threw her arms around him.

'Careful,' said Barney. 'You'll get raspberry on you.'

CHAPTER THIRTEEN
TWO WONDROUS THINGS

On the computer monitor, Chas narrowed his eyes. 'What's going on? Who's that?'

'Hi, Chas,' said Barney. 'We're here to help.' He held up the silver locket. 'We can use this to open up a doorway to your universe. You don't need to overload the reactor.'

'Why, Mr Barney Watkins!' cried Chas cheerfully. 'What a pleasant surprise! I do hope you're enjoying the use of your EGG now it's been returned to you. You should have brought it with you. Would have given you something to do in the three minutes you have left before you die.'

Gill looked at the controls on the console. 'The reactor's overloading. There doesn't seem to be any way of stopping it.'

Barney nudged Gabby. 'What's got into Chas?'

'He's a lot more evil and selfish and horrible than we thought he was. Than *I* thought he was, anyway.' She took off her glasses and wiped her eyes with the back of her hand. 'Oh mate. I've been a total, total idiot.'

Barney nodded. 'You've been an absolute jerk, Gabs. No two ways about it.'

Gabby nodded dumbly.

Barney stared at her a long time, then his face softened. 'But these things happen, don't they? No point worrying about that now if we're about to get blown to smithereens. This is Gill, by the way.'

'Hi, Gill,' said Gabby. 'In case you're wondering what the four awful squidgy wobbly personlike things are, they're people who've been caught in a 4-D trap and made to look all squidgy and wobbly by Chas.'

'Thought it might be something like that,' said Gill.

Barney addressed Chas on the monitor. 'Look, mate. We can end this business without anyone getting hurt. Please. Show a little respect for us 3-D beings.'

'Respect?' said Chas. 'You don't respect an ant when it crawls out in front of you. You just step on it and go on your way.'

'I don't step on ants,' said Barney. 'I like ants. They can carry stuff fifty times their own weight. They actually farm other species of insects the way we farm livestock. They're pretty cool. And so are we, when you get to know us.'

'You know a lot about ants,' said Gabby. 'I'm impressed.'

'Did a project last year.'

'Do you know why I did those magic tricks?' asked Chas.

'Is the answer because you're a repulsive attention-seeking bighead?' said Gabby.

'Haha,' said Chas flatly. 'I nearly split my four-dimensional sides. No. I did it for the challenge. Yeah, it was a challenge to restrain myself into doing stuff that small, that pathetic. I could have levelled mountains. I could have made your sun vanish. I could have turned this entire planet inside out like a sock. But no. I kept it small. That was what amused me. I was kinder to you ants than you realise.'

'And yet you still gave yourself away,' said Gabby. 'You couldn't just blend in with us human beings, could you? The stuff you did may have been small but it was still impossible.'

A siren blared. Gill looked at a read-out on the console. 'That's it. The reactor's overloading. We've got about thirty seconds.'

'Please, Chas!' cried Gabby. 'I'm sorry for insulting you earlier. *Please!*'

'Blimey,' said Chas. 'You ants aren't half boring sometimes. See you, losers.' The image of him on the monitor vanished.

Gabby and Barney stared at each other. Neither of them knew what to say. It occurred to Barney that he should probably hug Gabby, what with this being their last few moments alive and all, but the thought that she might not want him to nagged him. It also struck him as fitting that the last thoughts ever to flicker through his mind would be ones that were confused and a bit awkward.

'Open the locket.'

Barney seemed to snap out of a trance. 'What?'

'Open the locket,' said Gill. 'It's our only option.'

'But that won't stop the reactor from overloading.'

'No,' said Gill. 'But it might attract the attention of someone who can.'

Barney frowned. 'How do you mean?'

'We can debate the details afterwards – if there *is* an afterwards! Just open the damn thing!'

'OK, OK. How do–'

'Twist the two metal catches at the same time and press the little button on the back. Hurry! We'll be dead in a few seconds otherwise!'

'Right. Blimey. This thing is really fiddly, isn't it?'

'Just do it!'

'OK, OK. Ah, I think I've–'

The world suddenly became a much whiter, brighter place.

Outside, on Daisy's back seat, Dave saw a shaft of brilliant white light burst from one of the windows in the reactor complex. A shiver coursed through his body. It was exactly the same white light he had witnessed when Fleur vanished. However much his memory had deteriorated, he knew, he would never forget that.

A ghostly white owl that he had been watching flit from rooftop to rooftop for the past half hour took fright and darted silently away from the power plant. As it flew its movements seemed to slow to almost nothing, as if it were suddenly flying through treacle. Its great white wings froze in mid-flap and the bird hung motionless in the air.

Dave stared at the owl, his jaw slowly opening. Something very odd was happening.

Now there was more of the brilliant white light. It was pouring through what looked like a rip that had opened up in the night sky above the power plant.The rip lengthened, releasing fresh bursts of white light, becoming a twisting ribbon of unearthly energy.

Two enormous pointed shapes appeared through the rip, pushing their way into the universe, being born out of the night air itself. The rip convulsed and the two shapes emerged fully, revealing themselves to be two enormous cubes, both a full mile in length across each face and made from some weird grey jellylike substance that pulsed and shimmered in the starlight. The huge cubes floated silently towards Sanderling Ridge.

'Blimey,' whispered Dave. 'There's something you don't see every day.'

The two massive cubes came to rest in the air directly above the power plant, hanging there silent and still as the mysteriously frozen owl. For a few seconds, nothing happened. Then both cubes twitched, as if sneezing. There was a thunderous rumbling noise and two smaller cubes – each no more than a metre across – detached themselves from the main pair. These smaller cubes floated silently and without hurry down towards the reactor building from which the white light was streaming. When they reached the

top of the control complex, they passed straight through the flat roof as easily as ghosts and vanished within.

His heart pounding, Dave clambered into the front seat of the car and twisted the key in the ignition.

In the main control room, the white light suddenly snapped off. Gill, Barney and Gabby blinked at one another until their vision returned to normal.

'Whoo,' said Barney, rubbing his eyes. 'When that light was shining I put my arm over my eyes and I could actually see the bones it. Powerful stuff, that Harland radiation.'

'Harland radiation?' said Gabby, steadying herself against the control console.

'It's caused by the gravitational ripples that accompany the opening of a gateway to a higher dimension. I've been reading up on it. Gill and Dave have loads of notes on weird stuff.'

'Wow!' said Gabby. 'Someone's really done their homework!'

'Sorry to interrupt,' said Gill, 'but I can't help but notice that we're all, y'know, *still alive*. What's happened to the reactor?' She examined the dials and read-outs on the console. 'Funny.' She tapped one with her finger. 'Doesn't seem to be responding at all. I wonder why.'

'It's because there's been a localised rip in the fabric of space-time,' came a voice from behind them. 'Time has slowed almost to nothing here at the plant.'

The three of them turned around in unison to find Dave standing in the doorway. Gill flung her arms around him. 'Hello, darling! How did you get in here?'

'Just walked past the security guards,' said Dave, shrugging. 'They all seemed to be wrestling on the floor downstairs. Didn't even notice me.' He smiled warmly at Gabby. 'You must be Gabby. Rufus was telling me all about you.'

'Who's Rufus?' asked Gabby, frowning.

'Me,' said Barney. 'Dave's not terribly good at names.'

'And they,' said Dave, motioning to the four columns of grey-pink awfulness, 'will be some people caught in four-dimensional snares, I take it? Fascinating!'

'Great,' said Gill. 'Glad your mind is being stimulated by all this. Shall we all sit down and have a seminar about advanced hyper-geometry – or shall we try to figure out a way that we can all go home? My back and legs are killing me. I haven't moved this much in twenty years.'

'I guess whether we leave is up to them,' Dave said.

'Who?'

He pointed upwards to where two greyish cubes were floating gently down from the ceiling like children's helium balloons being tugged on a string. The cubes slowed their descent and hovered in the centre of the room at roughly head-height.

Gabby gasped. 'What on Earth ...?'

With a click, the computer monitor switched itself on. Chas's smug face filled the screen. 'Nothing on *this* sad little speck of a world. These creatures are from an infinitely vaster realm. The one I inhabit. And boy – are you in trouble now! These things are even more powerful than me and they won't like the way you've tried to keep me captive in your crumby little universe.'

'Who are they?' asked Gabby, breathless.

'My mum and dad,' said Chas. 'Well, two of them.'

'Two of them? How many mums and dads have you got?'

Chas screwed up his nose in thought. 'A little over three thousand, I think.'

'Three thousand mums and dads?' That seems–'

'Rather a lot? Yeah, I suppose it is, compared to you 3-D beings. Things are a bit more complicated where I come from. Each hyperbeing has several thousand parents, each one being partly male and partly female.'

'That must be a bit confusing.'

'It's a nightmare when it comes to remembering birthdays.'

Gabby's eyes suddenly blazed. 'Hey! What was that rubbish you were just saying about us keeping you captive here? That's rich! We'll be glad to see the back of you!'

'Enough of your lies now, underbeing,' said Chas coldly. 'MumDad 357 and MumDad 2961 don't want to hear your snivelling. I expect they'll just want to crush this world into a radioactive cinder and then we'll be on our—'

As Chas was speaking, one of the floating cubes pulsated and a spark of white energy flew from one of its corners towards the computer monitor. When the spark touched the screen, something extraordinary happened. Chas's mouth began to shrink as he was talking, his voice growing rapidly quieter, until his mouth vanished entirely, leaving a completely smooth patch of skin under his nose. Noticing this, Chas glared and shook his fists.

Now the two cubes shimmered and began to soften, melting and re-forming until they had formed themselves into two approximately humanoid shapes. Their features were blurred and indistinct. They looked like a pair of clothes shop mannequins to whom someone had taken a blowtorch. Rough, squelching mouth-holes tore themselves open in the figures' heads. They spoke in unison and their combined voices sounded like water swirling down a plughole.

'Good evening, creatures of this 3-D realm,' gargled the hyperbeings. 'Forgive us this intrusion into your dimension. We've taken the precaution of lifting this area of your planet out of space-time for a little while. It will prevent us from being noticed by your fellow creatures and allow us a modicum of privacy while we deal with this matter.'

'Umm, hello,' Barney ventured.

Dave and Gill were clutching one another, both open-mouthed in silent awe. Dave waved limply.

'So what's going to happen?' asked Gabby. 'Are you going to destroy us like Chas said?'

The hyperbeings shook their heads and waved their crude, semi-formed arms emphatically. 'Absolutely not,' they said in unison. 'You must ignore the pronouncements of the one you call Chas. He is what you would call on this world "a total div".'

'A total div?' repeated Gabby.

'Is that the right word?' asked the hyperbeings. 'How about "twit"? "Lamebrain"? "Dimwit"? You get what we're trying to say. He exhibits foolishness on a grand scale.'

On the screen, Chas gesticulated furiously, his face turning red.

'That's putting it mildly,' said Gabby. 'He nearly destroyed everything within a thirty-mile radius.'

'Chas is a mere child,' said the hyperbeings, 'and a difficult one at that. He's scarcely a thousand years old. We left him partially inserted in your universe the way you might leave a baby in a playpen – out of harm's way for five minutes while you make a cup of tea, as it were. We thought your world would be an amusing distraction for him.'

'You gave him our world as a *toy*?' said Barney. 'Billions of people live here! Don't you think that was maybe a *teeny* bit irresponsible?'

The hyperbeings shifted uncomfortably. 'We did not expect him to be so *rough* with you and to try to escape. For that we apologise. Though your lives are incredibly short and your mental horizons incredibly narrow, you still have value and should be treated with respect.'

'We know that!' exploded Barney. 'Of course we have value! We don't need some blobby know-alls from another universe to come down here and patronise us.'

'Ouch,' said one the hyperbeings. 'That hit home.'

'Yeah,' said the other. 'Fair enough. We've messed up here pretty badly. We're sorry for the trouble Chas has caused. He's been a pretty lousy ambassador for us up here in four-dimensional space. Is there anything we can do to make amends? We'll stop your reactor from exploding and free the people in this room caught in 4-D snares – that goes without saying.'

Barney looked at Gabby. 'I don't think we need anything from the fourth dimension. I think we've had more than enough of the place, to be honest, haven't we?'

Gabby nodded and looked down at her shoes.

'There is something, actually,' said Dave. He was

holding on to Gill's hand very tightly. 'We have a request. For information ...'

One of the hyperbeings pointed an unfinished fingerless hand at Dave. 'Yup? What is it?'

'We lost our daughter over thirty years ago. We suspect she was drawn into your universe. Is there any way of finding out if this is true?'

The hyperbeings listened, nodding in unison. They replied with one voice. 'This happens from time to time. Freak gravity whirlpools can erupt when bridges between universes are created. Tidal forces can disturb objects near the entrances to the bridge. Things can get rotated, turned inside-out, even. Or sucked inside.'

'Can you tell if that happened to Fleur?' asked Gill.

'Let's see. We'll need to scan you for DNA matching.'

A white spark jumped from the head of one of the hyperbeings and whizzed through the air towards Dave and Gill. It buzzed rapidly around the elderly couple like a mosquito and then zipped back to the hyperbeing's head. The hyperbeing cocked its head on one side, as if processing some information.

'Ah,' it said. 'Fleur Abbott?'

Dave and Gill gasped. Gill put a hand over her mouth. 'Yes!' said Dave excitedly. 'Fleur Abbott! Do you have any information about her?'

The hyperbeings exchanged a look. 'We do. She is indeed in the fourth dimension.'

'Good God!' cried Dave. 'After all this time. Our little Fleur. I can't believe it! Tell us more. Tell us, please.'

'When a being from your universe enters our own,' the hyperbeings began, 'the 3-D being undergoes a process of change as it grows itself a 4-D body, enabling it to move freely in hyperspace. This can take several thousand years, as you would understand it. We have detected the brain pattern of your daughter. She is living in our universe and undergoing the changes necessary to thrive there.'

'Is she all right?' asked Gill. 'She's been all on her own in there for thirty years!'

'Could she come back to us?' asked Dave. 'Appear to us like you or Chas?'

The hyperbeings considered. 'Why don't you ask her yourselves?'

'*What*? What do you mean?' Dave and Gill were clutching each other for support, their hearts pounding furiously.

'Fleur does not yet possess the skill to penetrate into your universe from ours. This is why she has been unable to contact you since she disappeared. However, as there is a locket bridge already open here between our dimensions, we can allow her to communicate with you through us.'

There was a *squeeeeech* noise. Grey jellylike matter poured from the stomachs of the two hyperbeings, who began to shrink. The matter formed itself into a torso, arms, legs and a head and soon there were three (somewhat smaller) hyperbeings there in the control room instead of two.

The new hyperbeing walked unsteadily towards Dave and Gill, arms outstretched. The elderly couple looked horrified, unable to reconcile this nightmarish form with the little girl they had lost so long ago.

'Mum! Dad! Hello.'

She sounded many years older, the lilting voice of a little girl replaced by a woman's confident tones, but Dave and Gill knew instantly that it was her.

'Fleur! Fleur! Our little Fleur!'

On wobbling legs they rushed to embrace the grey featureless figure, but their arms passed straight through as if it were made of steam.

'Damn matter frequencies,' muttered Dave.

'Fleur, darling!' said Gill. 'I can't believe it's really you! Are you OK? How have you been? Has anyone been taking care of you?'

The grey figure put a thoughtful hand to its chin. 'It's funny, Mum. Sometimes it feels like I've been gone years and years and years and then sometimes it feels like it was just five minutes ago that we were in the park and Dad was telling me about the Wandering Knight. Several thousand MumDads adopted me! They've taken good care of me. Oh, Mum, Dad – there's so much to see here. It's amazing!'

'We've missed you so much,' said Gill. 'It was like our lives ended the day we lost you.'

'It's OK,' said Fleur. 'I'm here now.'

'Yes but for how long, darling? Won't you have to return to the 4-D world soon?'

'That's true,' said Fleur. 'I will. But that doesn't mean you can't come back with me.'

'*What?*' said Dave. He turned to one of the

other hyperbeings. 'Is that possible? Can Gill and I go into your universe?'

'Sure!' said the hyperbeing, perking up. 'We'd be delighted to assist in your passage to the fourth dimension.'

'No problem whatsoever,' said the other hyperbeing. 'Be nice if something positive came out of this incident.'

'Permanently?' asked Gill.

'Sure. Why not?'

'Oh,' said the first hyperbeing. 'Just thought of something. I'm afraid you folks may not like it.'

'Oh what now?'

'Well,' said the first hyperbeing, 'the thing is, once a 3-D being enters four-dimensional space permanently, its 3-D body decays while its new 4-D one grows. This means the bodies you inhabit now will be cast away and you will acquire a completely new physical manifestation.'

'These old bodies of ours will be thrown away?'

'Yes. I'm afraid so.'

Gill and Dave burst into laughter. 'Can we have that in writing, please?' said Dave and they laughed again.

'Fleur,' said Gill, 'we're coming back with you.'

'Hooray!' cried Fleur and waved her grey, stumplike arms.

'Good,' said the first hyperbeing. 'That's settled. Are you ready to go now?'

'Right now?' asked Gill.

'This gateway won't stay open forever. It might be now or never.'

'It'll be so great,' said Fleur. 'We can be together! There's a whole bunch of *really* cool mysteries in the fourth dimension. You're going to like it there.'

The Abbott family embraced one another, ignoring the fact that one of their number existed at a different matter frequency and couldn't actually touch the other two. This state of affairs would soon be remedied.

Gill and Dave turned to face Gabby and Barney.

'Thank you, Geek Inc.,' said Dave. 'This wouldn't have been possible without you.'

Barney flushed. 'Oh, you know. No big deal. Happy to help, eh, Gab?'

Gabby nodded. 'It's been interesting,' she said and laughed nervously.

'And let me tell you two something,' said Gill, 'there's no shortage of mysteries in Blue Hills. Scratch the surface and there's a whole world of weirdness underneath. And it's there, waiting to be investigated. Take it from us, the Society of Highly Unusual Things.'

Barney and Gabby exchanged a glance and both silently mouthed the word 'wow' and giggled.

The first hyperbeing looked at the second. 'Well, no point hanging around, is there, MumDad 2961?'

'Quite right MumDad 357,' said the other. 'Let's be on our way. Avoid the traffic.'

There was a succession of white flashes. First the mouthless, gesticulating Chas vanished from the monitor. Then the three Abbotts exited the 3-D world forever in a single brilliant burst of Harland radiation. Finally, with a wave of their crude, unfinished hands, the two hyperbeings slipped back into their own incredible realm.

The silver locket rattled to the floor, its two halves snapping shut.

Barney and Gabby stared at one another in wordless astonishment. There was much she wanted to tell him, but before she could say any of it, Orville McIntyre burst into the room with his men and had them arrested.

CHAPTER FOURTEEN
INTO THE NIGHT

The sleek, dark vehicle raced along the deserted road towards Blue Hills, powerful headlights glaring, tunnelling its way through the night. Ahead, a lone rabbit hopped softly on to the tarmac, watching with huge brown eyes as the approaching yellow light grew steadily bigger and brighter. *The moon*, it thought in its simple way, *is behaving very strangely tonight*. The car thundered directly over the rabbit, its two sets of roaring wheels passing either side of the quaking creature. As the vehicle's lights receded into the distance, the stunned rabbit bounded swiftly back to its hole, hoping that the moon would be in a better mood tomorrow night.

On the car's back seat, their hands bound by plastic ties, sat Barney Watkins and Gabrielle Grayling, talking in low voices so as not to be heard by the car's driver. Gabby's face was streaked with tears.

'I can't believe how stupid I was to be taken in by Chas,' she murmured. 'I can't believe how stupid I was to want to leave everything and everyone I know to go to some stupid fourth dimension. But most of all I can't believe how stupid I was to *call you stupid.*'

'I believe the phrase you used was "you moron",' whispered Barney with a grin.

'Oh mate! I'm so sorry.'

'It's OK. Really. I *was* a moron. *Am* a moron. Fancy not knowing Sherlock Holmes is a fictional character. I had to find out sometime, I suppose.

It's the Easter Bunny all over again.' He chuckled quietly.

'But you were clever to get help from Dave and Gill. And brave to come and try to rescue me. You're better than Sherlock Holmes, Barney. You're real.'

Barney felt his face glow. 'Yeah, well. You'd've done the same, Gab.' He shifted uncomfortably in his seat and tapped on the tinted window screening them from the driver. With a motorised whir, the screen retracted a few inches, revealing the red cap of the military policeman in the driving seat.

'What is it?' asked the driver gruffly.

'When are we going to get home?' asked Barney. 'Assuming you're going to let us go and not lock us up in a dungeon somewhere.'

The driver snorted. 'Think you've been reading too many thrillers, son. We'll be stopping off at the police station at Philpotton soon. Mr McIntyre has commandeered an interview room. He wants to have a little word with you about tonight's shenanigans.'

The two kids groaned. Orville McIntyre had subjected them to a similar interrogation after the Gloria Pickles incident. It had not been enjoyable.

'And then?'

'Then we'll take you straight home. Your parents have been informed that you're helping out on official government business so they're expecting you to be late. That all?'

'Yup.'

The motorised window whirred shut.

'Great,' muttered Gabby. 'That means we won't be home for hours.' She bit her lower lip and stared out of the window at the bleak moonlit moors.

'You can be sure McIntyre will want to know all about the fourth dimension so he can try to exploit it for the government,' said Barney grimly. 'But we can't risk another inter-dimensional incident like tonight's. We ought to tell him to steer well clear of it. It's far too dangerous.'

Gabby did not reply. Her eyes were still transfixed on the dark and desolate landscape sweeping past them.

'Gab?'

'Mmm?'

'You OK?'

'Mmm? Oh. Yeah.' She didn't look at him and chewed thoughtfully at her thumbnail.

'What's wrong? You've gone all silent and mysterious.'

'I was just thinking. It's probably nothing. When you and Gill arrived in the control room you said something.'

'I said several things, I'm sure. Most of them either pointless or obvious, if the past is anything to go by.'

'No, I'm serious.' She turned to face him. She was wearing an odd, puzzled expression. 'You said, "It's OK, Gab. We're here now".'

'OK. So what if I did?'

'And you had all that yucky raspberry stuff on the front of your shirt.'

'Most of it's still there. My favourite school shirt, too. All my others are dead scratchy. What about it?'

'You looked a bit like a robin redbreast.'

Barney guffawed. 'A very large, confused one, I'm sure.'

'No, listen!' She touched his arm. 'I had a dream the previous night. Well, that morning, really. About a robin redbreast. You remember the one with the robot? Like in the kid's telly programme that Fiona Cress was telling us about?'

'Like the statue?'

'Yeah. And in the dream the robin redbreast said, "It's OK, Gab. We're here now," just like you did. *Exactly* like you did. Isn't that weird?'

Barney shrugged. 'Weird, yeah. But it's a weird *coincidence*, innit?'

Gabby chewed her thumbnail again. 'Mmm.

You're probably right.' She paused. 'Probably.'

Barney smirked. 'What? Are you saying you can predict the future in your dreams now, Gab? Not like you to leap to the craziest explanation. I thought you were supposed to be the rational, scientific one.'

She raised her eyes. 'I know it sounds wacky. It almost certainly is wacky. But the sense of déjà vu when you came in the room was almost overpowering.'

'Well, you know what you have to do, don't you?'

'What?'

'Test it. Keep a dream diary and see if any of it comes true.'

Gabby laughed, her face brightening. 'Great idea, Vice-Pres! An experiment! I will. You are a genius. I always said it.'

In the front seat of the vehicle, behind soundproof tinted glass, the driver touched a control on the dashboard, lowering the volume of

Gabby and Barney's conversation that was being fed to him by a secret microphone, and which he had been monitoring since the start of the journey. He touched another control and a ringing tone sounded in his earpiece. After a few rings, Sir Orville McIntyre answered.

'Good evening, Captain Grebe.'

'Evening, sir. Thought you should know something about the Grayling girl. Ahead of your conversation with her.'

'Is this to do with the hyperchild?'

'No, sir. Something else.'

'Oh goody. Do share.'

'May possess some level of precognitive ability. Possibly able to dream about future events.'

'Ooh! A dream prophet! That would be juicy. It would certainly tie in with what we know about her father's abilities. I shall make a note in my jotter. You've done very well, Captain Grebe.'

'Thank you, sir. Just doing my job.'

'And doing it splendidly. Goodnight, Captain Grebe!'

'Goodnight, sir.'

In the passenger seat of the other limousine, which was thundering along the empty roads just ahead of the one containing Gabby and Barney, Sir Orville McIntyre removed a tiny spiral-bound notebook and a fat gold fountain pen from the inner pocket of his pinstripe jacket. With one he wrote a few brief sentences in the other and returned them both to the pocket. He jabbed a fat finger at a button on the dashboard in front of him. The tinted screen separating the front of the limo from the rear retracted a few inches.

'About time!' snarled an angry female voice from the back. 'You can't do this! This is kidnapping! I want to speak to a lawyer! Stop the car!'

'Hush, dear lady,' cooed McIntyre. 'Save your

breath. I think you'll find that I can do whatever I wish and only seven people in the entire world could possibly prevent me.'

'What are you blathering on about, you fat fool?'

McIntyre chuckled. 'Oh, Miss Goosefoot! You really are one of the most appallingly poisonous and foul individuals I have ever had the misfortune to encounter. You have the brain of a cornered serpent and the manners of an enraged pig. You are self-centred, self-serving and self-seeking. You are a painful wart upon the thumb of humanity. You are, in short, dear lady, one *nasty* piece of work.'

Julia Goosefoot rolled her eyes. 'I *know*.'

McIntyre smiled. 'How would you like to work for me?'

The following morning Gabby awoke feeling refreshed. Pulling on her dressing gown, she stumped to the bathroom, a slow yawn creeping across her face. The water from the tap felt icily cold and invigorating as she brushed her teeth. With her free hand she placed her glasses on the end of her pointy nose and studied her face in the mirror.

Was today a school day? She tried to remember. She had got up at the usual time when her alarm went off, just in case. In her head she went through the days of the week ...

Suddenly she gasped and sprayed a shower of white foam over the mirror. She ran back to her bedroom, wiping her mouth on her sleeve, and picked up the notebook and biro resting on her bedside cabinet while the dream was fresh in her mind. Hastily she scribbled, her brow furrowed intently.

Gabrielle Grayling's Dream Diary – November 8th

I dreamed of Blue Hills in ruins. I dreamed of the streets I grew up in reduced to radioactive rubble. I dreamed of my school destroyed. My house a blackened shell. Choking smoke and ashes everywhere. Not a living thing in sight. The sky forever black.

She paused and took a deep breath before she added the final line.

And it was all my dad's fault.

EPILOGUE

Somewhere beneath London, an experiment was taking place.

In a brightly lit white-tiled laboratory, a balding man with a very large nose watched as two teams of scientists fussed around and prodded two enormous, identical machines. The machines were great humming, whirring things made of gigantic metal coils and strange rubbery protuberances. They looked a little like hi-fi speakers and a lot like weird, futuristic engines. There was one at either end of the laboratory and they were joined by a single, quite thin, cable.

Also, in the centre of the laboratory, in a large metal cage, there sat a dog – a beagle. It was a youngish creature with long floppy ears and big dark eyes that were wide and alert. Despite its imprisonment in the cage the beagle was cheerful, its tail waving happily from side to side like a car windscreen wiper and its nose furiously atwitch.

One of the scientists nodded to the man with the very large nose. The man with the very large nose smiled and made a neat tick on his clipboard.

The door to the laboratory burst open and two people strode into the room. One was a young, tubbyish man in a pinstripe suit, the other a tall blonde woman.

In its cage, the beagle sniffed the air curiously.

'What news, Edgar?' asked the man in the pinstripe suit.

'All systems functioning and ready to go, Sir Orville,' said Edgar, adjusting his thick-rimmed glasses on his frankly gargantuan nose. 'I've been working night and day on this. Good job I'm a single man as I don't know who'd put up with the silly hours I work.'

'Fabulous, fabulous!' beamed McIntyre. He gestured to the blonde woman beside him. 'This is Miss Goosefoot. She is my new –' he paused '– actually I cannot tell you what her job title is as it is classified beyond your security clearance. Suffice it to say she works for me and is new.'

'Charmed,' said Edgar and held out his hand to Julia. Julia stared at it as if it were a headless mouse that a cat had just vomited at her feet. Edgar withdrew his hand, unshaken, and put it away in his pocket.

'As I say,' McIntyre went on, 'Miss Goosefoot is new so I would be grateful if you could give her a quick summary of today's proceedings.'

'Certainly, Sir Orville.' He jerked a thumb at the two strange machines. 'Here, miss, we have two Harland capacitors capable of absorbing radiation. To put it in simple terms, they work a little like a bath sponge—'

'Yes, yes,' Julia interrupted. 'You don't have to treat me like a complete idiot. I was in charge of a nuclear fusion reactor until last week, you know. I expect the Harland capacitors work by absorbing neutrons. Am I right?'

'Indeed you are!' trilled Edgar. 'Forgive my oversimplification! I had not realised you were so knowledgeable in this field. Yes, the Harland capacitors absorb the radiation that is produced when a gateway is opened to a higher dimension. This makes the gateway more stable and gives us much greater control. Within each machine is one of a pair of special angel lockets we have obtained. Angel lockets – you will no doubt know – are the objects in which these gateways are traditionally kept. The two we possess are unique as far as we can tell in that they both open gateways to the identical point in the fourth dimension. This means they are effectively joined together. Put something in one locket and it pops out of the other, no matter where the other is. We've not actually been able to do this in the past because of all the nasty Harland radiation getting in the way and attracting the attention of the hyperbeings who live in the fourth dimension – a rather snooty, patronising lot if you ask me. But now – thanks to these shiny new machines – we believe we can successfully move something through the fourth dimension and make it appear elsewhere. Hence the presence of our volunteer today, Toby.' He nodded at the beagle in its cage.

Julia narrowed her eyes. 'What use is a wormhole through four-dimensional space if you need these two massive machines at either end? Hardly convenient. If you're transporting something you'd probably be better off sticking it in the back of a van.'

'If this test is the success we think it will be,' replied Edgar, 'we can quite easily reduce the size of the machines to something more manageable. Tiny even, potentially.'

A small smile creased the corner of Julia's lips. 'That's more like it. You want to be able to post a letter to the leader of a foreign nation and when he opens the envelope for a whole army to come pouring out of it through one of your gateways.'

McIntyre gave an impressed whistle. 'You have to hand it to her, Edgar. It's like she has a PhD in Applied Viciousness from Thug University.'

'I'll have you know I'm entirely self-taught,' said Julia coyly.

'Shall we start the experiment?' asked Edgar.

McIntyre smiled warmly. 'By all means, old boy.'

Edgar knelt down and unlocked the cage holding Toby the beagle. 'Come on,' he said brightly. 'There's a good boy. Who wants to be a pioneer in dimensional transportation, eh?' He pointed at the two machines. 'You're going to go in that one, Toby, and magically appear a second later at the other one! Won't that be fun!'

Julia wrinkled her nose. 'I'm not sure I like this, Orville.'

McIntyre nodded. 'I agree entirely. Look, Edgar. Julia and I are both really quite keen on dogs and we're not sure you have the right idea about this experiment.'

'Oh?' said Edgar. 'What do you mean?'

McIntyre cocked his head to one side. 'The thing is, old fellow, if the experiment is a rip-roaring success with young Toby here, we're still going to have to test it with a human being before we risk sending two thousand of Her Majesty's most highly trained troops through it. Sensible thing to do seems to me to cut out the middleman – or middledog as it is in this case –

and jump straight to testing it with an actual person. Do you follow?'

Edgar nodded cautiously. 'We could do that. But it might take some time to find a willing volunteer at this late hour. It's still a potentially very dangerous experiment for someone to submit to, to say nothing of the legal implications present in—'

'Here's another idea,' interrupted McIntyre, cheerfully pulling a revolver from his pocket and training it directly at Edgar's heart. 'How about you test out the system right now and I don't fire bullets at you? What do you say?'

Edgar nodded grimly.

McIntyre waggled the revolver and Edgar took up position next to one of the machines. A scientist turned a dial and the humming noise intensified.

Toby barked happily and bounded over to Julia, who tickled and stroked his long floppy ears.

'Can I keep him?' asked Julia.

'Why on Earth would you want Edgar?' asked McIntyre, perplexed.

'Not him, the dog,' said Julia. 'I like beagles.'

'Oh, I see!' McIntyre shrugged. 'Yes, I don't see why not. Man's best friend and all that.' He gave a thumbs-up sign to the nearest scientist. 'OK! Throw the switch!'

The scientist threw the switch.

MORE BOOKS FROM
MARK GRIFFITHS